PRAISE FOR

ATTITUDE

"The author's grasp of the complexities of the young mind in *Attitude* is realistic and engaging. The diversity of the characters reminds the reader of today's society and likens to the analogy *Let the best man win*. But the best man may not be the person you had in mind." —Donna Kirk, Author, *Finding Matthew*; Stories published in Canadian journals, newspapers and in American newspapers.

"*Attitude* is a fast-paced novel pitting resourceful teens, Lyle and Laura, against a cast of quirky, dysfunctional characters and real bad asses who mostly get what's coming to them. This story will quicken pulses and is bound to please readers of YA novels." —Michael Joll, author *Persons Of Interest* and *A Time To Love And A Time To die.*

"Dave Moores has combined all the elements of the genre: rebellion, friendship, relationships, first love, angst and identity into a dark, twisted coming-of-age drama that puts us in the head of the protagonist like few authors have done. Hats off folks. A strong, new voice in YA literature has arrived on the scene. Hopefully more from this author is in the works." —Ray Holmes, author *Witnesses And Other Short Stories.*

"A surprise at every turn of the page. Dave Moores captures the very essence of teenage angst in *Attitude* and never fails to impress on the reader, that these, above everything else, are also *people*: warm, intelligent and vibrant." —Ken Puddicombe, author *Racing With The Rain* and *Junta.*

"Smart, quirky, and full of tension, Attitude is one of those novels where the characters stick with you long after you finish the book. Moores is a skillful writer who gives them all depth and authenticity and brings them to life in a way that is nothing short of remarkable." —Catherine McKenzie, author of *The Twisted Minute*

UPCOMING FROM DAVE MOORES

Sparkles And Karim

ATTITUDE

A Novel

Dave Moores

MiddleRoad | Publishers

"Making Literature see the light of day."

Library and Archives Canada Cataloguing in Publication

Moores, Dave, author

Attitude

ISBN 978-1-9991365-8-1 (soft cover)

Front Cover Photograph courtesy of

Marlene Ford

Cover design by Ken Puddicombe

"It's not my fault I can't be like you, okay? I don't get up in the morning thinking the world is one big, shiny, happy place, okay? That's just not how I work. I don't think I can be fixed."
— **Lauren Oliver, Author,** *Before I Fall*

DEDICATED

To my granddaughter Natalie, whose wise and witty observation sparked the train of thought that led to this story.

We were discussing Star Wars.

"Does Han Solo have The Force with him?" I asked.

"No," she said, "he has attitude and a gun."

Table of Contents

ACKNOWLEDGMENTS

I wish to express my particular gratitude to Brian Henry and the members of his writing forum, in particular beta readers Shauna Clinning, Donna Kirk, Lyanne Matcham and Catherine McKenzie, for their encouragement and astute advice.

Lately I am especially grateful to the folk at MiddleRoad Publishers for sharp editing and a guiding hand.

Above all, and as always, my profoundest thanks to my dear, incomparable wife, Chris.

1. ATTITUDE AND A GUN

"You want clean underwear, Lyle? Get yourself out of bed and do your own laundry for once. The machine's still there in the basement — it hasn't moved." At the time Lyle'd ignored his mother like always, but now, headed home from school into Southmead, kicked out early for attitude, again, he found himself wishing he'd listened up.

"I'm not going to your stupid gym class," he'd snapped at Ms Wynne, "I told you already, I can skip it any time 'cos of my sore leg, so get out of my face." Smirks from Troy Thomas and his posse. They knew, the losers. Too bad — no way Lyle was about to strip for Phys Ed in the briefs he'd been wearing for days.

Lyle was skinny-tall, sharp featured and dark eyed. Untidy black hair curled around his ears. The bullies at Southmead High knew to steer clear. Not so Ms Wynne. She hustled him along to the office quick enough to make his head spin.

"Last chance, Lyle," the Principal told him. "This is completely unacceptable behaviour. You're fifteen years old," — like, he didn't know that? — "any more of it and you'll be facing suspension, you hear me? Now apologize to Ms Wynne, get yourself out of here and come back tomorrow with a better attitude."

Lyle wasn't sure which he despised more, the school as a crap institution staffed by losers, or the Principal and his lame threats. He coughed deep in his chest and horked a greener into a snowbank.

His boots made squishy-crunchy sounds in the slush swept to the curb by the morning's plough. A low overcast crawled above and casual big snowflakes spiraled down. Out here beyond the town's meagre limits, the snowbound desolation of Huron County stretched in every direction. Only the wind turbines broke the stillness, like stranded aliens, Lyle often thought, signaling for a ride home with their slowly revolving blades.

He came up on the random sprawl of small-time commerce that lined the road before Southmead's downtown — a Mister Lube, Al's Budget Plumbing, those kinds of places. Next, a row of run-down cottages. The occupants weren't much for clearing sidewalks, so Lyle kept to the roadway. Past the final cottage stood the PetroCan station where – big surprise, not – Lyle spotted his wingman Garth Priest patrolling the forecourt, a habitual hangout chosen for no reason Lyle could fathom. Garth turned from staring into the middle distance and fixed his gaze on Lyle.

"Kicked out early, were you?" Garth's brown eyes and square, open face were made to smile but they never did. He only showed up at school when so inclined, got away with it on account of his Asperger's. What a crock.

Lyle ignored the question and fired back one of his own. "Hey, what's up, fool?"

"Nothing." The two of them wandered into Southmead's three-block downtown, ranks of weathered yellow brick storefronts, quite a few dark, with *For Lease* signs in the windows.

"So where are you headed, my esteemed friend, this excellent afternoon?" Garth asked. He always talked like that.

"Home, dumbo, where else? But I gotta pick up a can of mushroom soup. Mom's doing her grey chicken again tonight, barf."

They'd been buddies since forever. Garth didn't buy Lyle's bad boy act like the other stupid kids, didn't call him on it either, just ignored it. Lyle was cool with that but Garth was kind of different. Being the son of the town's funeral director could do it. That and the Asperger's.

The somber afternoon had streetlights coming on. Garth grabbed Lyle's arm. "Oh, look, here comes your best friend, Miss Laura." Laura MacDonald was nowhere close to being Lyle's friend, which Garth knew perfectly well— the smart ass.

The fur trim of her hood exquisitely framed Laura's face with its alert blue eyes and expressive mouth. Lips that would bear a sly smile as she pulled you in for a kiss — like that was ever going to happen — and she had the belt of her puffy jacket cinched above the swell of her hips. She paused outside Van Beek's Hardware and started poking at her phone.

In a weird way Laura reminded Lyle of an angel he'd seen on a stained-glass window in a rare visit to church. Not the serene, blank-faced kind though. This one was a vigorous spirit wielding a sword, letting demons have it.

"Hi Laura," he said, "lookin' good today. On Fleek."

Laura glanced up as if startled, though she had to have seen them coming. A snowflake caught on her cheek and Lyle, on a crazy impulse, reached out to brush it away. It was the briefest touch. He badly wanted to do it again.

She flinched and screwed up her face like she'd stepped in something. "What are you doing? Get off me!"

"You had a thingy on your face there."

"Never touch me, okay? Sheesh! So why are you out of school today, Lyle Prince, as if I couldn't guess?"

"How come you aren't in school yourself?" Lyle replied, counterattack being the best form of defence.

"None of your business."

Garth gave his friend a sharp elbow in the ribs and muttered, "Monthly cramps probably, nimrod."

Lyle recovered fast. Running into Laura out of school was an opportunity, albeit stupidly small. "So Laura, you want to go for pizza?" He noticed a sprinkle of tiny freckles across the bridge of her nose.

Mom's cash for the soup, plus the toonies he'd liberated from her purse, ought to cover a pizza. She'd give him shit but he'd close his ears to it. Laura switched attention back to her phone. The whistle and rumble of the CN freight sounded from the tracks north of town.

Laura looked up. "What did you say?"

"Pizza?"

"Eew no, all that gross melted cheese."

Oh, come on. He'd watched her inhale a slice of four-cheese pizza in the lunchroom only last week. Why did girls say these things they'd so obviously made up? Because they could, hello.

A strand of red-gold hair fell across Laura's left eye and she pushed it back. "Gotta go, guys."

"Shall we be favoured with your presence in school tomorrow?" Garth said.

"Ha ha, funny boy, like you're ever there." She turned to cross the street toward the PharmaPlus and Lyle caught a waft of fragrance like the flowers in Grandma's garden. He felt a tug, close to physical hurt.

Their eyes followed Laura as she disappeared into the store. A slow-moving pickup swished by on the wet pavement. Pizza with Laura? In your dreams.

The sting of rejection had Lyle itching to do something scary, way better than routine shoplifting. He remembered Dad, incarcerated in Milton this past year. Some days he missed his father and some days he didn't, but Dad had taught him stuff.

He shoved Garth into the laneway between Van Beek's and the Mini Mart. "Forget lifting a few crummy Reece's Pieces, stupid Park forgets to lock his side door half the time. There's gotta be darts in there."

"So you're smoking now? Since when?"

"Nah, for the money, dough brain. Lee and his buddies'll take 'em." Garth turned down the corners of his mouth. Lyle shot him a pitying grin. "Come on, you little chicken," he gave Garth a buddy-punch in the shoulder, "let's do it."

The Mini Mart's side door opened with a turn of the knob. A smell of cleaning fluid, racks of cartons labelled Raisin Bran, Tide, Campbell's Soup — there you go, Mom — and, jackpot, cigarettes of many brands. Lyle was into it now, a buzz and a tension across his chest, like the time, out of audacity or pity, he was never sure which, he'd picked up a rock and bashed in the head of a rabbit he'd found half-dead in a trap.

Garth's harsh whisper: "How do you propose we carry this stuff?"

"Garbage bags, find garbage bags, quick! And we'll sneak out down the back lane in case Wowchuk comes by in his cruiser."

A door slammed somewhere close. A thump followed by shouts came from the front of the store. "On the floor, now! Don't fuckin' move!"

Garth's eyes went wide. He jigged from one foot to the other, hugged himself and began making low humming noises. Lyle had seen this before. One time, a stray pig had wandered into town overnight, sliced its leg open on a garbage bin, and run around bleeding. Garth had freaked out at the blood and commotion as a choice sample of the town's youth, hooting and laughing, set out to capture the frantic pig.

Lyle gripped his friend's elbow and hustled him, firmly but not roughly, to the side door. "You go home now," he said. Garth started shaking his head. Lyle grabbed him by the shoulders and looked him in the eye. "No, get outta here. Catch ya later." He shoved Garth out the door and closed it quietly.

A swing door separated the shop from the storage room. A glass pane at the top of the door, no more than a foot square, installed for providing safe entry and exit, had a crack running from top to bottom. Lyle peeked through.

A tall skinny guy in a ski-mask was at the cash drawer, his back to Lyle. An accomplice stood over the proprietor, Mr Park, who was on his back beside the magazine display — blood dripping from his mouth had spattered on his shirt.

The bozos were giggling and calling to each other—on something, by the looks of it, Meth perhaps, the pair of losers? How dare they muscle their way into Lyle's very own local corner store and mess up his adventure? He scooted back to the side door, opened and slammed it twice, loud, propped it open and snuck behind a rack of Doritos boxes.

Sure enough, Bozo Number One hustled in, spotted the open door and made for it. Lyle moved fast, not caring if the guy heard or saw him, dashed into the store and went for the top left drawer beside the cash.

Yes! It was there, only a little .22, a toy compared to Dad's Glock, but they all worked the same way. Lyle took hold of the gun and felt the weight of it. Loaded.

Number Two spun around. "Aw, little boy, don't mess with that thing. You're only gonna hurt yourself."

From his position at the end of the counter, Lyle had a clear field of fire across the store. He raised the gun, pointed it at the guy's face and cycled the slide to chamber a round the way Dad had taught him.

The eyes in the ski-mask went wide. "Hey, hey hey," the guy shouted, "Mitch, get back in here for Christ's sake!"

Bozo Number 1 pushed through the door from the back. His jaw dropped. "What the fuck? Ah, jeez, Brad!"

"Alright, assholes," Lyle's voice came out high but not losing it, "on the floor, now."

Neither one moved. Mitch burst out, "Brad, for Christ sakes . . ."

"SHUT UP," Lyle yelled. "On the floor or I swear one of you gets it. Who's gonna be first? Mr. Park, go outside and find us some help here."

As the proprietor rose unsteadily to his feet, red and blue flashes lit up the store. Enter Sergeant Wowchuk, heavyset, weapon out, belligerent. Right behind him, Laura.

The cop pointed his gun. "Get down you two. Don't move. Lyle, drop it."

Lyle dropped it.

"What in God's name have you gotten into, you dumb kid? Having a little disagreement among yourselves? Like father, like son, I guess. How did you get mixed up with these two?"

"Officer," pleaded Laura, "he's not with them, honest. We met on the street outside, like, a minute ago."

No way. Laura MacDonald, wide-eyed and a little bit breathless, was right here standing up for him.

Mr. Park spoke up, too. "She right. He save me, he hero!"

Wowchuk was silent for several seconds. Then, "Get over here Lyle, and you two, ski-masks off, now!" He pulled out his phone, called for backup, then started cuffing the Bozos.

That done, the cop gave an exasperated shake of the head. "Alright, I guess I have to revise my assessment, kid. These gotta be the same two clowns that knocked over the corner store in Howick last week. And as for you young lady, didn't I tell you to stay outside?"

Laura didn't answer. She moved to stand beside Lyle. The flush of winter cold was on her cheeks and there was the aroma of flowers again. Unbelievably, she grasped his arm. "I saw these guys go in and I heard shouting, so I called the station."

Lyle had aspired to be a badass but the perks of law enforcement were looking good right now. "Laura," he said, "I owe you big-time. Sure you won't change your mind and come for a Pizza?"

There was mischief in her smile, curiosity too. It made his knees go weak. "Well maybe, but omigod, Lyle, that was amazing, what you did. What's going on with you?"

He shrugged. "Attitude, I guess. Attitude and a gun."

She moved close. "You're bad," she whispered, her breath warm on his neck.

*

By the time Officers Leach and Jensen showed up, a knot of gawkers had gathered outside the Mini Mart, whispering to each other. They exchanged knowing looks as Lyle and Laura emerged with Officer Leach. The force's other cruiser was nowhere to be seen so *The Bozos* got bundled, not too roughly but not too gently, into Cruiser 1. Lyle and Laura would have to make it to the Station House on foot with the officer. As the car door was closing, one of the Bozos, Mitch, spotted Lyle in the group heading off to the Station House.

"You're gonna be sorry, kid," he yelled, "you have no fuckin' idea what you're gettin' into."

Lyle turned to answer but Laura stepped in front of him. "Please Lyle, you did good. Leave it. You're not the only one involved in this." An intensity like radio waves shimmered off her, then it passed. Why did girls always want you to back off to avoid trouble? The prospect of pizza with Laura was looking so-so.

Laura, Lyle and Mr. Park, escorted by officer Leach, entered the station. Lyle was no stranger to Southmead Police Department. The station, formerly a liquor store, stood a few steps off Main Street in the remnants of Southmead's only try for a shopping plaza. The force comprised Nora, the civilian office manager and dispatcher, Chief Marlon Harrington, Sergeant Wowchuk, three constables and two special constables for, what else? Special duties.

At the reception counter, the Chief, a substantial presence, grey buzzcut, gun on hip, looked totally ready to come down hard on any and all instances of petty crime, civil disturbance or mindless driving. "Sit here you two," he told Laura and Lyle, "your parents will be here anytime."

Lyle figured Harrington had learned the hard way to go by the book so no smart-ass lawyer could get interview notes thrown out. He was still pumped but not expecting to be in trouble. There was the gun though. Would he have fired it? He might have.

Seconds later Judy Prince blew through the door. She gave no sign of being here to support her son. Her expression said it all — what had the little shit done now? A compact woman in weathered jeans and parka, her helmet of blonde hair showing some grey, Judy looked ready to rip into anybody who might cross her path. Her face carried the imprint of hard times and she clearly expected more of the same today.

Sergeant Wowchuk had to have sensed her state of mind. He intercepted Judy before she got to Lyle. "Ms Prince, thanks for coming out. Last thing you needed, I'm sure. Your son's not in trouble, okay? But we need you to be present when he's interviewed. It's procedure."

Judy caught sight of Laura sitting beside Lyle. "What's she doing here? Is somebody going to have the common decency to tell me what's going on? My god, I totally don't need this, I truly don't. Procedure, you said? Well, let's get on with your *procedure* because I have orders to process. Ah, Jesus, Lyle, can't you stay out of trouble for once?"

Lyle stared at the floor and stayed mute. Meeting Mom's gaze would only make things worse.

Wowchuk took Judy's elbow. "Let's go sit over here Ma'am, and I can give you the general picture if you'd like." He glanced at the Chief. Harrington nodded. It wasn't hard to tell he'd be happy to leave the task to his sergeant.

A funk of mortification settled over Lyle. Mom was doing her typical wig-out in front of everybody, with Lyle's new friend sitting right beside him. She was going to mess things up for him, like always.

Wowchuk's quiet words appeared to calm Judy but then, "A gun? My boy had a gun! Oh, my god, I don't believe this, tell me you're kidding, that's not possible!"

Lyle sank further into himself. The room went quiet.

The sergeant's attempts to pacify Judy were interrupted as the front door of the station admitted another parent. Plum lambskin jacket, black leggings, an older but by no means ageing version of her daughter. The woman looked around, her expression full of horror at finding herself in this place.

Laura jumped up and the two embraced. "Oh sweetheart, oh dear God! Your father's on his way. Don't worry my darling, whatever you've done, he'll sort it out, I promise." Her gaze fell on Lyle, who'd been sitting next to her daughter with every appearance of companionship. Horror changed to the look of someone faced with a piece of roadkill. The woman pulled her daughter to the other side of the reception area and the two began an intense whispered exchange, along with the mother's frequent dismayed glances at Lyle.

Next stop, the interview room. The Chief, Lyle and his mother, sergeant Wowchuk and a recording machine, Chief Harrington asking the questions.

"Lyle, you're not in any trouble, but I'm required to ask you, Ms Prince, if you want a lawyer present."

Judy raised her eyes to the ceiling. "Where am I gonna find a lawyer at this hour, and who's gonna pay him — you?"

The Chief's chair creaked as he shifted his bulk and smirked. "Sorry Ms. Prince, legal aid don't cover a situation like this, when no charges have been laid. So it's up to you."

Judy blew out air. "Go ahead, ask him what you want. But there's a problem later, its not gonna be a beautiful day in the neighbourhood, Chief."

Harrington let it go. His nicotine stained fingers toyed with a ballpoint. "So Lyle, where were you in the Mini Mart when you realized there was a problem?"

The lie came easily. Dumb cops, Lyle knew this was coming. "Over in the grocery section, looking for a can of soup."

Judy broke in. "That's right, I sent him to pick one up so I could do supper. I make a chicken casserole, it's one of his favourites."

If she only knew. Kenny used to like it though, and Dad, before he went to jail.

The Chief ignored the interruption. "So what happened then?"

"There was yelling and banging. Somebody shouted *Get on the floor.*"

"Go on."

"So I peeked around the shelf back there. Mr Park was on the floor with blood on his face. A guy was standing over him, and the other one had his hands in the cash."

"And what did you think about that?"

Judy leaned forward. "Lyle, don't say nuthin'. Chief, doesn't matter what he thought, I been through this kinda stuff with you lot before. Just ask what he saw, please and thank you."

Harrington shook his head. "Only trying to establish a framework, Ms Prince."

"Yeah, well, establish your framework all you want. Ask him what he saw, alright?"

"Do you mind if I ask him what he heard?"

Lyle'd had enough of this testy interchange. "Mom, can I talk now?"

Judy nodded. "Remember what happened to your father." She fixed Harrington with a glare that spoke plainly of past confrontations over Dad's arrest. The Chief turned to Lyle and motioned him to proceed.

"The guy guarding Mr Park was getting antsy, telling his buddy to hurry it up. But then the other one jumped like he heard something, and he went off through the door to the back. I was stuck where I was. To make it outside I'd have had to go right by the bozo keeping an eye on Park. And they shouldn't ha' done that to Mr Park. It wasn't right! So I ran along behind the shelves to where the cash is."

This next part might be tricky. "Look, I knew he kept a gun in the drawer there, okay? Everybody knows about it."

Well not everybody, but word had gone around. "So I grabbed the gun out of the drawer, and the other guy came back and I told them both to get on the floor, and then Officer Wowchuk arrived, and Laura."

Harrington nodded, but then he leaned back and fixed his eyes on Lyle.

"Uh, Lyle, were you ever in the storeroom?"

Here we go. Lyle remembered Dad telling him, *Always look 'em in the eye. Then they think you're telling the truth, the turkeys.* Lyle locked eyes with the Chief. "No, I told you where I was."

"Only, back in the cruiser, one of the detainees told my sergeant you were in the back room."

"No."

"Why would he say that?"

"I dunno. Maybe high on somethin'?"

Judy spoke up. "Do not cross-examine my son! He's a witness, not a suspect. Was Mr Park in the cruiser when the guy said this?"

"No."

"Well, go ask him, why don't you?"

No, Mom, no! Alarm clenched Lyle's guts. Sergeant Wowchuk hauled himself to his feet and left the room. Lyle had no idea what to say or do.

A prickly silence lasted until Wowchuk's return a couple of minutes later. "He says he doesn't remember, couldn't see from where he was on the floor. Thought Lyle must have come in the front door."

Major surge of relief. Had Park, the guy he'd been set to rip off, decided to pay him back a big favour or was he simply confused, halfway out of it? Lyle didn't know what to think, and he didn't like not knowing.

A familiar sense of frustration replaced the relief. Nothing he did ever turned out quite right. He always felt he could have done it better, smarter. Why was he always down on himself this way? He didn't know that either, another thing he didn't like.

Harrington simply shook his head. "Well then, I guess we're done, for today anyway. Thank you both, Lyle and Ms Prince. I can't see much of a problem with Lyle using the gun. But you were stupid, Lyle. You should have stayed where you were. What if one of them had got the gun off you? So no more messing with guns, hear me? You of all people should know the trouble they'll get you into. We'll write up a statement and you can sign it tomorrow before the Court proceedings. Nora will call with the time. Okay, Ms Prince?"

So that was it? What about, *Way to go, kid!*

"Whatever." Mom replied, "Come on Lyle. It's too late to cook now. You want a pizza?"

The irony. On their way out Laura threw Lyle a conspiratorial roll of the eyes. Her mother, now supported by a tall, good looking man who Lyle recognized as Dr McDonald, gave Lyle the hairy eyeball. He'd see them all again tomorrow. How was that going to go?

2. NEXT UP

A dazzling blue day, minus fifteen, the sun barely up at 8am. Ice crystals borne on a blistering northwester glittered in the air, conjuring sparkling rainbows above the road.

Judy had no eye for these fleeting displays. She'd fed Diesel the cat, yelled at Lyle to get up and shower, and headed out for work. She wheeled her Toyota pickup — rimed in road salt, three hundred thousand on the clock and showing it — onto the crumbling asphalt behind her store. It looked like Earl had come by and cleared the snow with his Bobcat, but the night's hard freeze had left icy ridges. A busted ankle was the last thing Judy needed.

Not long past fifty, Judy had a tight, working woman's body and the helmet of yellow hair. There had been a time when the look in her pale eyes said, "You think?" Which encouraged a certain type of guy to guess the worst they'd get in return for a proposition was a smart-mouthed putdown. They might do a lot better. The look had gone missing a long while ago.

Judy unlocked the back door of Southmead Auto Supplies, dumped her coffee and breakfast sandwich on the bench, kicked off her boots and hung her parka. Another morning chasing orders and stocking shelves, then court with Lyle this afternoon. She'd seen this movie before.

When the Canadian Tire closed, Judy, a section manager, had gone for it. With help from Monty Priest, old flame and father of Garth, she'd scraped together the capital and credit to open her business. She carried the low unit-price stuff: lubricants, antifreeze, anything in a spray can. The expensive items she'd take orders for, but Amazon was eating into that lately. Still, it paid the bills, or had.

Lyle. Hardly a word out of him last night. The usual one-shoulder shrugs and surly silences. Judy supposed teenagers were bound to be like this but

Lyle was different in ways she couldn't put her finger on. For a start, he looked nothing like his birth father, whose identity she'd never tell a soul. Instead, the dark colouring, deep set eyes and sharp cheekbones conveniently reminded people of her husband, Art. Plenty of girls would go for that look — she had. But the resemblance was a mixed blessing with Art in jail and five years still to serve for armed robbery.

The landline's ring cut short Judy's train of thought. She checked the call display. Hank Niles, goddammit. She asked herself where it had all gone wrong. The way it looked now, her life amounted to a bunch of loss, screw ups, and failed hopes, her remaining living son an aimless near-dropout and her business on the brink of closure, thanks to Hank.

*

Unlike his mother, Lyle was grasping the morning as an opportunity not to be missed. Word of the foiled heist had travelled all over, typical of Southmead. A cluster of fascinated kids, pretending not be fascinated, had gathered in the schoolyard. Feet stamping, hands in pockets, they feigned indifference but stayed in earshot as Lyle related an edited and enhanced version of his story. Garth was nowhere to be seen.

The arraignment would come later at two pm. Nora had called early to confirm a preference for having witnesses present in case the magistrate had issues. They needed a signature on Lyle's statement anyway, *So kindly come on down.*

"So Lyle," Troy Thomas again, "quite the fun time. Get wrecked, eh? Wanna be my bodyguard, bet you'd like that, dude?"

Lyle made an as-if face. "Wonder what you'd ha' done, bro? Crawled in the corner and wet your panties?" Guffaws from the audience. "And when Laura showed up, she was like, *Oh that's so cool Lyle, what you did.* I slayed it with her. She'll be all over me now, you watch."

Troy took his eyes off Lyle. A derisive grin came on his pudgy face. Lyle turned to look. Oh crap, Laura had shown up around the corner of the schoolhouse with her bestie, Darlene. Their stony expressions said it all. They'd heard of course, idiot.

*

Judy picked up the phone. "Good morning, Judy." The whiney, mocking voice of her store's landlord, Hank Niles. "I hate to bug you," yeah right, she thought, "but I need your decision, sweetheart. I have investors waiting on me."

Judy felt slimy things creeping up her legs. How she could ever have found this fat fuck remotely appealing floored her.

"And that email of yours. I don't appreciate threats. Why don't you just close up, sell the inventory and get a job at the canning plant? That store's never gonna pay its way, 'specially at the new lease rate. I'm doing you a favour, sweetheart."

A vein throbbed in Judy's temple. No way was she going to sell the inventory at five cents on the dollar and go to work at that shit hole. It would be hard, sweaty work and her hip was bothering her. Hank wanted her out. He owned a block of three stores on Main Street and Judy's was the middle one. It was an open secret that Harpers of Southmead, the clothing outlet down the road and one of the town's few thriving businesses, was after Hank about leasing all three so they could knock through the walls and make one big store.

"Don't call me sweetheart and go fuck yourself, Hank. You want me gone? Bring it on. You see what happens."

His reply came out breathy and shaky. "One last time, Judy. Your lease is up. Pay the new rate or the eviction notice will be on the door next week, along with a padlock. Your call. Sweetheart."

Judy slammed the phone down. It started ringing again.

*

Lyle and his mother pushed through the plate glass doors of the courthouse, crossed the small atrium, headed down a hallway paneled in blond wood, and entered the courtroom. The place was less than a quarter full. Its two front rows were occupied by a legal-looking crowd, mostly well-dressed middle-aged guys who appeared quite at home. The remainder of those present, perhaps twenty in all, sat in closed-off groups, relatives or supporters of those in trouble, Lyle supposed, and oh, there was Laura with her mother and father. She had her red-gold hair up in a knot and Lyle couldn't take his eyes off her despite dirty looks from the parents. Lyle's mom preferred seats near the back. The room displayed a tense solemnity, people conferred in hushed tones, few smiles, the robed woman up front, the high ceiling.

It wasn't Lyle's first time here. He'd been brought up for shoplifting and got lucky. They'd treated it as a summary offence and let him off with a caution to never, ever, appear here again. But that was Juvenile Court. This was a new cast of characters and a different script.

Mom whispered to Lyle, "That's the Prosecutor Gervaise, he brings the case to the Magistrate, Bernadette Paulson, her up there, and that lady's the Clerk of the Court who kind of calls the plays." She'd know this stuff from being here for Dad.

The door at the back opened and Mr Park stepped in, accompanied by a younger woman, a daughter possibly. His face bore the results of yesterday's beating. The Crown Attorney broke off a muttered conversation with Chief Harrington, beckoned to Park and found him a seat near the front. Lyle saw the Chief glance over to where he sat with Mom and point him out to the attorney.

Paulson rapped the gavel. "Next up."

The Clerk of the Court, a solid woman in her fifties, dressed in a well-tailored grey suit, read from an iPad. "Next case before the Ontario District Court of South Huron. Docket number one one seven nine three. The Crown versus Mitchell Bigelow. Attempted robbery and one count of assault and battery."

The Clerk nodded to Harrington, who in turn signalled to a side door. Bozo Number 1 entered handcuffed, escorted by Sergeant Wowchuk. Lyle did a doubletake. The guy looked almost respectable! Somebody'd got him a haircut, shaved his blond stubble, and put him in a decent shirt. But the cold eyes and tattoos up the neck told a different story.

After various preliminaries and a summary by Chief Harrington of the evidence supporting the charges, Bigelow declared his intention to waive legal representation and enter a plea of not guilty.

"Mr Gervaise, your wishes?" Paulson asked the Crown Attorney.

"The usual, Your Honour, bound over in custody, a flight risk, no bail."

The Magistrate shifted her derriere to the other cheek. "So is there anything you want to say, Mr Bigelow?"

"Plenty, Your Honour, it's a total setup! We went in the store to get smokes and that kid over there shows up out of the back. Like what was he up to in there, you might wanna ask, then he comes up with a gun and starts waving it around. He's the one who oughta be stood here, not me. He had to have been on a break-in, then he tried to put us in the frame. It's bullshit!"

Lyle started to rise but Mom gripped his wrist and held him down. Magistrate Paulson pulled her spectacles to the end of her nose, raised her eyebrows and stared at the Crown Attorney.

Gervaise gave a dismissive shake of the head. "We have statements from all the witnesses, in particular Mr Park here — note the state of his face, Your Honour — that Mr Bigelow and his accomplice assaulted him and were in the process of robbing the Mini Mart. I respectfully submit that no further evidence is required to demonstrate who is telling the truth here. My recommendation stands."

Paulson paused to scribble notes. She looked up, fingered her chin, and addressed her Clerk. "Janet, only two more today, right?"

"Correct Your honour. The other accused from this incident and finally, a DUI."

"Good. I'm curious. Can we hear from our young gunslinger?"

Judy gripped her son's wrist again. "Shit!" she hissed, "Go on, get your ass up there and for Christ's sake don't go mouthing off!"

Lyle stood. Was he about to get caught after all? He'd thought he was in the clear. The Magistrate addressed him. "Is the lady with you your Mother?" Lyle nodded. The indignity of getting shepherded around like a five-year-old burned his cheeks.

The Magistrate looked over at Judy. "Mom, is it okay with you if we hear your son's story? I won't put him in the box, I'm, well, like I said, curious."

Judy nodded.

"Is that a yes, Ma'am? We need to hear it."

"Yes."

Lyle walked to the front and Janet positioned him sideways-on, facing both the room and the Magistrate's bench, well clear of Bigelow — still cuffed but with a derisive sneer on his face.

"And your name is?"

"Lyle Prince." Lyle thought he'd better add, "Your Honour." So he did.

Guided by questions from the Crown Attorney, Lyle gave the same account as he had at the station yesterday. Nobody challenged it, though Bigelow muttered under his breath and was sharply told to be quiet. Lyle took care to look the Magistrate in the eye. Mr Park backed him up and Lyle knew, with a surge of nervy relief, that he'd got away with it. Attitude ruled.

What was more, Laura, along with her parents, had just heard his story in full for the first time. He didn't know what that would mean but nothing bad, surely? He took good care to thank Laura for calling the cops, though after this morning's disaster in the schoolyard, he doubted it would make any difference. Still, he returned to his seat pumped.

Mom gave him a tight smile but it said, *You and I are due for a frank discussion later, mister.*

A tall, fleshy-faced man, ginger haired, sharp blue suit, rose to his feet. "What does *he* want, the prick?" Judy asked, half to herself. Lyle recognized Billy Niles, Manager of the local Farmers' Co-operative, brother of Hank who owned Mom's store.

Paulson regarded him, expressionless. "Good morning, Mr Niles, do you have an interest in this case?"

"Your Worship, if you will consider bail for Mr Bigelow and his companion, I am ready to provide the funds. I know these two and I'm perfectly confident in making this offer. And frankly, I have real concerns about the way this has all gone down. Mitch has a job he could lose if you put him inside. He needs to support himself and pay his rent. You're taking his livelihood away. This is all being handled wrong, in my opinion."

Niles' looks and petulant demeanour reminded Lyle of Alec Baldwin on SNL who did a killer impression of the U.S. President.

The Magistrate raised a finger. "Mr Niles, your comments on court procedure are out of place. Kindly retract them." A stare down followed until Niles shifted his feet and looked away. "Pardon me, Your Worship, no disrespect intended, I take it back."

"Thank you. And Mr Niles, it's *Your Honour* not *Your Worship*. Mr Gervais, do you still prefer incarceration?"

"Most certainly, Your Honour, for the reasons I already gave. Witness intimidation is a particular concern, given the accused's demonstrated propensity for violence."

Lyle couldn't believe they were considering releasing the guy. Dismay gripped him. Bigelow's threat as they'd left the Mini Mart was all too clear in his memory. And worse yet, now the guy knew about Laura's part in his capture. No way! He wondered if he was allowed to object. Put up his hand like in school. Yeah right, they'd think he was a retard.

The Magistrate took another moment to add to her notes, then took a breath. "The Crown's concerns regarding release on bail are not unreasonable. Nevertheless I will grant bail but, Mr Bigelow, do not approach or contact any of the witnesses here today. Do so and the bail money will be forfeit and you'll be back inside. Release on bail is granted. The bail amount is set at fifty thousand dollars."

Billy Niles' eyebrows shot up. "What! That's totally…"

Paulson brought down her gavel. "Next case."

Lyle and Mom made it to the atrium and were headed for the door when a petite young woman of colour in a trim emerald green pantsuit approached, giant sunglasses shoved above her forehead.

"Marigold Wallace from The Huron Beacon, may we have a quick word?"

Lyle saw a chance to salvage some celebrity and, before Mom had a chance to object, he extended his hand. The woman's grip was firm and warm. Her voice had the sing-song lilt of the islands and her large, dark eyes zoomed in on Lyle — he thought he could easily get lost in them. Black people were still a rarity in the county and this, his first encounter, piqued his curiosity and made him want to know more of her.

"Ms Prince, your son spoke well in there, I'm sure you're proud of him."

Mom was plainly not up for this. "There's nothing to add, Ms Wallace. We need to get going."

No way was Lyle about to take off but he didn't want to come across too eager. "Mom's right, we need to make this quick."

"Okay, we will. Mr Prince, were you scared?"

"Please call me Lyle. No, I was more pissed off, sorry, I meant to say angry. There's too much of this bullshit petty crime around here. I mean, I guess there's always gonna be shoplifting and stuff, but to smack the poor guy around? No way! That was when I figured, enough. I mean, you have to take a stand, don't you?"

Where had that come from? Was it more of his bullshit, or did he actually mean it? Marigold seemed to like it. Mom regarded her son with trace of incredulity but he was on a roll. "So I did what I had to do, and here we are."

The reporter nodded. "I get that, I do. Another quick question. The young woman who called the police, is she a special friend?"

"Not at all, I just know her from school. I owe her, though."

The woman flashed a mischievous grin. "Do you plan to find a way to thank her?"

This was not a direction Lyle wanted to go. He could picture the headline:

YOUNG LOVERS FOIL SOUTHMEAD ROBBERY,
DETAIN PERPETRATORS

"I dunno. Maybe."

Marigold had a final question. "I'm in Southmead to check into an outbreak of unusual incidents in the last couple of months. Livestock missing, vandalism, threatening notes in mailboxes. Has your family experienced anything?"

Mom cut in. "No, not at all. It's a bunch of nervous old women blowing stuff out of proportion. Excuse us now, we have to go."

Lyle was taken with Marigold's open manner. "But if something crops up, we'll let you know."

"Why thank you Lyle." She dug into her purse. "Here's my card. Let's keep in touch." Mom rolled her eyes and hustled her son to the door.

***

In the truck. "You were in the back room like the guy said, weren't you? You lied and got away with it, you little bugger."

Been nice if she'd at least waited to get home before grinding his gears. He couldn't be bothered to keep up the deception. "Yeah, Mom, I was in there, okay?"

"You and who else?"

"Nobody."

"See, Lyle, there you go again. Lie to the cops if you must but not to me. Garth was there too. He told his dad and Monty called me, desperate to keep Garth out of it. Garth said you shoved him out the back door, which was the one smart thing you did in this whole mess. I can guess why you were there, so don't feed me any more of your made-up crap."

Lyle balled his fists inside his pockets. "Mom, you should'a told me before this!"

Part of him wanted to find Garth and punch him out, but he knew he never would. Garth told things as he saw them, always had. Only last week, in front of way too many listeners, he'd come out with, "Lyle, time for a shower my friend, you have excessive body odour."

"Why should I tell you?" Mom said, "Were you gonna give them a different version today than what you told the cops yesterday?"

"Oh sure, Mom, like how smart would that have been? But what if Garth's told other people?"

"I squared it with Monty. Garth will button his lip. Monty promised."

"He better."

"Forget Garth. Don't you know how close you came today, lying in court? It's too much, Lyle. You gotta stop with the shoplifting and all the other shit I don't even want to know about. I got my own problems." Judy horsed the truck through the turn into Mary Street and home. Number 79, a tired mid-century bungalow, stood apart on its scrubby five-acre plot outside Southmead.

Lyle had to get out of here before his head exploded. He'd known it for a while. There must be a way. He couldn't see it yet, but he would. Stuck in this crappy little town with a mother who never had a good word for him, and an oddball his only true friend, something more had to be out there, and one day he would find it.

In the driveway, "I gotta run over to the store." Mom told him. "Let yourself in and feed Diesel." She reversed onto the street and took off.

Lyle dug in his pocket for the front door key, then paused to check the sky. The day had turned dark with the threat of more weather, snow squalls off Lake Huron set to roll in like smoke across the empty fields.

3. THE KEEP

Billy Niles drove through town fuming. He wished the absolute worst day of her life on that bitch Magistrate and he knew his troubles today were far from over. The happy news of another hundred grand on the line of credit would have Clara taking a head fit. Billy was well aware of the speculations about his lifestyle, the mansion on five acres, the BMW, Clara's Porsche. It all came at a price well beyond the reach of a Co-op salary, and his second source of income was under threat from that damn reporter woman sniffing around. Something would have to be done about her. Or maybe not, because by next week the money worries would be over, just so long as Charlie and his crew didn't blow it. Some scary unpredictables in that bunch.

Billy turned in at the Curling Club and parked the Beemer next to his brother's '56 Thunderbird. Hank drove the T-Bird and his other classic, a metallic blue '62 Caddy DeVille, year-round. Billy found this incredibly dumb. Get salt in the frame of those old cars and you'd be looking at astronomic dollars.

Neither of the brothers went to the Curling Club to curl. In recent years the game had been appropriated by fit women in stretch leggings and boy did they stretch well, the pants and the girls both. Curling had become a spectator sport for the Niles brothers, armed with a double shot and a comfortable seat behind the glass.

Billy entered the club. He savoured its familiar smells of old wood and wax polish. The building had begun life as a World War One airplane hangar. Dismantled and shipped to Southmead in the thirties, its trusses and beams displayed a comfortable solidity, functional yet full of character.

A double rye in hand, Billy signed the bar chit and wandered over to where Hank had snagged their usual spot, a table by the window overlooking the rink. Hank wore his customary black and red warmup suit, another source of secretly held derision to Billy, as Hank, at three hundred pounds, was about as far as you could get from being an athlete. With a huge round head and a skim of darkish hair, full faced and blessed with lips like two slivers of meat, Hank looked nothing like his brother.

Too early yet for any action on the ice. The bar was close to empty as well, which made it a good place to discuss certain plans. Hank turned, raised his glass and they clinked. Billy sat and took a pull at his Crown Royal. The drink burned satisfactorily in his throat. He needed it after forking over the bail money for those two morons.

"Guess who I saw today in court?" he said, "Your old girlfriend and her shitbag son." Billy described the courtroom developments and nobody came out unscathed. He decided not to mention the bail amount and subject himself to mockery. The brothers spent a few minutes dissing Judy, Magistrate Paulson and the administration of justice around here, then got to business.

"So we're set for Sunday," Billy said, "I can't risk somebody spotting me out there. Can you still run a couple of holdalls, like you promised? Some stuff Bigelow needs. I don't even want to know. They're in the trunk."

Hank looked away. "I guess so. But Bill, one last time, this is the craziest thing I ever heard. Are you sure about it?"

"Too late now, little brother, believe me."

*

Fucking Billy, Hank thought as he headed out to the T-Bird. And this plan…jeez, his brother was such a turkey. But then he always had been.

The storm hit on the way to the drop-off. Tiny flakes slanted down like fireflies in the headlights. No problem, Hank could handle it. Winter tires were a scam, in his view. All you had to do was drive with caution and use your goddamn brains. Stuck in a drift, spinning your wheels, winter tires wouldn't help. Start digging, sucker, or call a tow truck.

As expected, Hank found Charlie and a few others hanging out at *The Keep*, a barn twenty klicks out of town with an attached shed, originally an equipment garage, warmed by a loud propane heater. *The Crazies*, as Hank thought of them, had turned the place into a kind of half-assed clubhouse hangout, somewhere to drink, stoke their grievances, plot strategy and store essential supplies.

Hank dumped his cargo by the bar, accepted a beer and took a spot at the picnic table that served as the only seating. He decided to try one last time to save these sad fucks from themselves. "Charlie," he said, "you know what I think about all this. There are about a million ways it can go wrong. I can't understand why you don't get that."

Chicken Charlie Webb owned a chicken farm or, more correctly, an egg-production facility. He was a small man with a shiny face and bad teeth. His watery eyes gleamed with the fervour of someone close to the edge.

"You know how it is today, Hank. Even effn' McDonald's wants free-run or free-range. The processors are getting the message and only yesterday I lost another contract. Talk to the farmers around here. Same story. It's time to take direct action, Hank." His buddies leaned in, nodding. "Do the politicians listen? Sure they listen, around election time. Then they do squat. I been readin' about the farmers' revolt, back in eighteen-thirty-seven. Those guys had it right, we're gonna walk in their shoes."

Hank stifled a snort. Give me a break, he thought. Charlie and his cohort had a real beef but, in his opinion, they were talking themselves into a frenzy and headed for disaster. Occupy the Sunrise Foods canning plant as a protest? Out of their minds. These guys would take Billy and the Co-op down with them. When it all went sideways, which it was bound to, they'd tell on Billy in about a minute. Madness.

The door blew open with a gust of cold air and snowflakes. Brad Watts and Mitch Bigelow stomped in. Billy should have left these two clowns in the clink where they couldn't screw things up further. They weren't even farmers, for Christ's sake.

Bigelow slapped Hank on the shoulder a little too hard. "Well hi, Hank, we're honoured. The brother of our fearless leader, no less."

"Sure, Mitch, from what I hear you'd be cooling your ass in the lockup right now if it wasn't for my brother. So mind your mouth, alright?"

"Hey, Billy knows who he can call on when there's business to be done. So I'll mind my mouth when I need to, Hank baby, oh yeah."

"Hey baby yourself, Mitch, keep Billy's name out of this. You know he supports you but he can't be associated with this scheme of yours. After it all goes down, you guys are gonna need his help real bad, so he has to stay clean. Think you can manage that?"

Bigelow mouthed an inaudible reply, looked like he'd been on the meth again. Hank let it pass and another round of Molson's got cracked open.

It went quiet for a while, then, "Hank," Mitch said, "you worry me, pal. You wouldn't, like, maybe, let on about our plans to the wrong people, would you? Since obviously you think we're out of our minds and all."

"Well, Mitch," Hank answered, "you're right about one thing. Yes I think you're all living in dreamland. But I'm not going to drop Billy in it, am I? So I won't be talking to anybody, okay?"

Mitch sniffed and did not respond.

Conversation took a turn towards the Maple Leafs' playoff prospects, but every so often Hank caught Mitch looking at him sideways.

Hank needed to get going. He went out back to relieve himself before hitting the road. "Coming down pretty good out there," he told the group on his return. He drained his beer, headed through the door and made for his car.

The T-Bird was Hank's favourite. He loved the Caddy too, but it was the Bird he'd take to cruise nights on summer evenings. He'd make it to them all, Owen Sound, Kincardine, Goderich. As he motored with the top down and the warm scents of the countryside in his nostrils, Hank sometimes asked himself why classic cars were such a big thing in Huron County. Time to tinker out here, he guessed, where life moved at a slower pace. A way to preserve memories of what, for many, seemed like a more secure, optimistic time. For Hank, it was a lot simpler. He loved the colours of these old beauties: the pinks, the turquoises, the creams.

Potter's Hill led down to the ravine. The road was getting slick. No anti-lock brakes on this baby, better take it easy down the slope. Whoa! Maybe he shouldn't have had that second beer on top of drinks with Billy.

4. WANT TO SEE WEIRD?

To Lyle's surprise, Garth had condescended to show up in the schoolyard despite bus cancellations after last night's storm. Courtesy of parental chauffeuring, Lyle assumed.

Lyle broke away from a half-hearted snowball fight and approached his friend, but he was in no mood for the customary exchange of insults that passed for greeting. "Bruh!" He asked, "why'd you tell your dad you were there at the Mini Mart? What were you thinking?"

Garth paused as usual before speaking, as if the circuits in his head were stuck. Eventually the answer came. "Dad asked me what I'd been up to that day, so I told him."

He may have lacked empathy, but there was nothing wrong with Garth's powers of recollection. No point screaming at him. Lyle decided on irony as the best way to handle this, though Garth wouldn't get it, probably. "I bet that went over well?"

"No, and he said some bad things about you. But then he told me not to tell anyone else."

"So have you?"

Another pause. "No."

"Will you? This is important, Garth. Friends gotta stick by each other."

"No. We still friends, then?"

This was a surprise. A good surprise.

The exchange was interrupted. "Wow, Lyle, looks like a real deep talk you're having with your weirdo sidekick. Anything we should know about?"

Oh great, Troy Thomas again, along with hangers-on Rick Morrison and Buddy Sauve.

Lyle turned, casual and easy. He walked over and halted nose to nose. Troy took a step back. Lyle spoke quietly, so only Troy would hear. "You ever call my friend a weirdo again, I will hurt you where it hurts the most. You won't be jerking off in the back of the bus for a while, guaranteed. You want to see weird? Go look in the mirror, you fat pig." He turned his back and rejoined Garth. "Jackasses."

In reference to nothing at all, Garth came out with, "Mrs Ellis, our next door neighbour, had her tires slashed last night. That's two on our street this week. And the McKinnons' cat's gone missing."

A lost cat, Lyle could understand. Coyotes got hungry this time of year. But Coyotes didn't slash tires. Marigold Wallace, the intriguing reporter had mentioned an outbreak of vandalism and petty theft. Now he had a reason to call her. Who could be doing this stuff, and why?

An outburst of surprised voices rose from the knot of vapers and smokers outside the gate. Lyle and Garth shuffled over. Lyle heard the name Hank Niles. That was the guy who wanted to kick Mom out of her store. Sharon Marsh was telling the tale. Her father'd got the call for his tow truck, Hank's car upside down in the ravine, his body wrapped around the windshield frame. Though hardly popular, the Niles Brothers were well known in Southmead, so this was a juicy bit of news. Lyle wondered what it meant for Mom. Maybe she'd be off the hook for the lease. He really hoped so— he knew she was worried stiff. Good riddance to Hank Niles as far as he was concerned. The bell rang for classes. No Gym today. Good.

*

A ways out of town on the Cranbrook Road, Jacob Ryan surveyed the blanket of snow on his driveway. Ploughing it out promised a tedious hour's work but nobody would go anywhere until it was done. He stomped around to the equipment shed, rolled up the door and climbed into the four-by-four. He'd mounted the blade last night, ready for the morning's task.

Jacob shook off the grumpy mood. Come on, he told himself, life here was good. His farm sat in a lazy bend of the Saugeen River west of Walkerton. The spread ran close to 300 acres planted with Soybeans, Canola and a bit of corn for the kids to sell at the front gate on summer weekends. It was a decent living and the Co-op kept things predictable. But not for everybody, Jacob thought, as he drove out of the shed. He was one of the fortunate ones. Talk of foreclosures went around all the time.

The Co-op was the lifesaver, for some at least. Quotas were established, prices set, permits issued, and the sale of your crop was guaranteed. Too bad if the food processing industry condemned the whole scheme as shameless price-fixing. Without a permit, the only way to sell your produce was on the black market at rock-bottom price.

Jacob saw himself as a practical man. Staunchly conservative in his politics, he nonetheless enthusiastically participated in the government-administered supply management scheme. The Co-op's dues were insignificant after all, paid monthly by bank standing order.

There were other costs, though. Four times a year, Mitch Bigelow would come by for a donation to the Farm Support Fund, no receipts, cash only. Give generously if you wanted your production permits processed in short order. No donation and the paperwork would disappear in the wheels of bureaucracy. Hadn't the Ministry of Agriculture in Guelph got wind of this? You'd think, but if they had, they didn't give a shit. Best to pay up and ask no questions. Once in a while, word would go around that someone had talked to the cops or the press. But then, for whatever reason, the rumour wouldn't come to anything. Jacob had heard whispers about certain merchandise available from Mitch as well, but he didn't want to know.

The meetings were cool, far from cordial. It was hard to be warm and friendly to a person holding out their hand for a wad of dollars in the customary plain brown envelope. Mitch was due to show up today, and Jacob planned to keep lookout and meet him by the road. He didn't feel comfortable letting the guy indoors.

Mitch arrived on time in his Ram crew-cab, black, dual rear wheels, the whole redneck shitkicker rig. Jacob had never liked the look of him or his truck. Pale eyes, small pursed mouth, straw coloured stubble. He put Jacob in mind of a feral creature, its face lined by unmet hungers. They exchanged brief greetings and Mitch brought the news of Hank Niles' departure from the World. "Gotta be tough on Billy. 'Course, they had their differences lately."

Oh, sure, how would Mitch know? The creep wanted Jacob to think he was one of the inner circle. Unlikely. Eager to end the encounter, Jacob pulled out the envelope holding his donation and thrust it at Mitch. "Here you go. The usual," he said with a pointed look, "mind you don't lose any."

Mitch flashed his usual scornful grin. "Yeah thanks for the warning, Jim."

"Uh, it's Jacob, not Jim. Jim's place is down the road a ways."

"Ah, shit, my bad." The guy cocked his wrist, index finger extended in a gesture which might, or might not, have mimicked a handgun, "So, Jake, a lot of funny stuff going on right now. You be careful too, buddy."

I'm not your buddy, asshole. One of these days somebody needed to bash the fucker's head in. Jacob turned away as the Ram blasted off, snow flying from all four wheels. The meeting had left him out of sorts. He needed distraction, boarded his own rig and went to finish the drive.

*

Lyle and Garth would eat lunch together the days Garth came to school. Garth got the hot dog and salad. Lyle, his usual burger and fries. They were about done eating when MaryLou Bothwell approached. Lyle was the last person Marylou would normally have anything to do with, nor he her, and he wondered what she wanted. She carried more pounds than the average and hung with a group big on poutine, Timbits, and Coke.

"Lyle," she said, "can I talk to you for a second?"

Lyle stood, made a face to Garth, and moved away beside Marylou.

"Now Lyle," she said, toying with her phone, her cheeks shaking in a way that had him backing off, "my mom doesn't want you all upset, okay?"

Nice of her, but it was hard to believe Marylou's mom would care about his emotional state. Come on, flab features, he thought, get to the point. Why did women always have to beat around the bush?

"Okay," he said, to move things along.

"Well, I got this call from my mom, you see. She was shopping in town and she saw a police cruiser pull up outside your mom's store."

Uh huh.

"And my mom said it may be nothing."

Lyle didn't respond.

"Anyway, they took your mom off in the cruiser and my mom told me she looked pretty upset. She thought you should know."

Oh shit. Damn right Lyle needed to know. "Thanks Marylou, tell your mom thanks too."

This was scary. New evidence about the Mini Mart episode, maybe? But why pick up Mom? Crap and double crap. Wasn't that all done with? While shoplifting and other acts of petty lawbreaking were no big deal, this was somehow different. It twisted his insides and he had to find out what was up, bad as it might be.

Back at the lunch table, he shared Marylou's news. Garth didn't hesitate. "The cops think your Mom killed Hank, of course."

Lyle laughed out loud. "Get out of here! Quit trying to freak me out. He drove off the road in the snowstorm, in case you didn't hear, and why would the cops look at Mom anyway?"

Garth lifted an eyebrow. "It's kind of a co-incidence, don't you think? I mean, you told me how he wanted her out of her store. Pretty convenient if you ask me. I bet she messed with his car. She fixed dad's brakes one time. She knows about cars, your mom."

Lyle had no time for Garth's crackpot theories. This was one of those moments when he dearly wished he had a phone. Mom had one of course, on the business account, and there were landlines at home and at the store, but the finances of the Prince household did not run to a phone plan for Lyle. He'd have found a job to pay for one, but part-time employment for teenagers was scarce in Southmead, and such jobs as there were went to families of business owners.

A favour he hated to ask. "Garth, can I use your phone?"

"Sure." Garth pulled his phone from a pocket and handed it to Lyle. The screen was black.

"Uh, is it on?"

"Yeah, go on, touch the screen."

Lyle was thankful that Garth had no sense of humour and wasn't one to make fun of people. He touched the screen and it lit up. There was a ton of icons, nothing like on Mom's phone. He couldn't even see how to bring up the dial pad. After more stumbles, and instruction from Garth, he managed to call Mom's number. A woman's singsong voice invited him to leave a message. He handed the phone back to Garth.

Trays in hand, a loud posse of girls approached, Darlene and Laura among them, headed to the empties cart. They came up on Lyle and Garth and the laughing and joking around stopped cold. They gave Lyle the same frozen look he'd received yesterday in the schoolyard.

Suddenly it all became too much. He picked up his own tray and flung it, complete with plastic plate and cutlery, to the floor. Head down, he ran from the lunchroom.

Backpack flung across his shoulder, Lyle exited the schoolyard,. Garth caught up, stepped in front and placed his hands around Lyle's shoulders.

Lyle raised his head and looked Garth in the eye. He didn't need this. "Take off, willya. You called my mother a murderer. That kind of help I don't need. Go on, lose yerself."

Garth didn't move. "No point in you heading home now is there? Come to my house. Dad will be there. Maybe he can help."

Lyle fought to breathe steady. What Garth said made sense, but making sense was not what he cared about at this moment. What he cared about, he didn't know. Right now he pictured himself walking out of town along some shitty little road into the frozen countryside and keep walking and walking...

"You should definitely come to my house," Garth said, "you appear disturbed."

A twenty-minute walk from school, Sunset Vistas Funeral Parlour adjoined Garth's house around a corner off Main Street. There had been an interment this morning, Garth told Lyle, and this afternoon a visitation was scheduled. Grandpa Millard had checked out at ninety-seven with fourteen great-grandchildren, a respectable score but by no means a record around here.

"Dad'll be busy for a while but come on in. May I offer you a beverage?"

Garth playing the gracious host? Whatever. Lyle hadn't shaken his funk, but the familiar surroundings of Garth's place felt okay. Worse places to be. Monty had a nice home here. Old red-brick house, fixed up good. It made the Prince bungalow look sick, with its dinged-up paintwork and grimy carpeting.

The pair sat in the family room slurping 7-Up. Ranger wandered in, a portly yellow Labrador-something cross, after treats. Garth greeted the dog and got lots of face-licks. Lyle had seen this before, how Garth and Ranger connected, seemed to know each other's minds. It was especially there today and watching the two of them told him something he hadn't quite grasped before. Locked up inside his withdrawn, undemonstrative friend was somebody not so different from himself.

But why hadn't Mom answered his calls? And as for Laura MacDonald, that was over before it had barely started.

5. WHEN YOU'RE DEAD

Home from school, Laura McDonald spent a few minutes letting Mom fuss over her and tell about her day staging the Murphy house — those people simply had no idea — then fled upstairs for the usual after-school texting.

Laura loved her parents but Mom's constant fainting-couch episodes over nothing drove her crazy. As far as she could see, Mom didn't treat her any different than she had five years ago, and the first time Laura had heard the term *Helicopter Parenting*, she knew in an instant what it meant. Thank goodness for Dad. He kept things bearable, would step in when Mom pushed her close to screaming.

Then there was the conflict, premature, oh please, over her future career. Mom thought interior designer, Dad saw medicine: nurse-practitioner for sure, and why not physician? Way too soon! Both careers appealed, but at fourteen, hello?

Her parents' relationship put her in mind of somebody caring for a much-loved pet. She wasn't sure how she felt about that. Mom was warm and kind, albeit subject to chronic anxiety but — and Laura hated to think this — not too smart. They'd have a family movie night, something suitable on Netflix, and Mom would ask obvious stuff, like, "Why did she get all upset when she found out her best friend called her husband?" It scared Laura a little bit, but then she'd tell herself this was way better than what some of her friends, Darlene for one, had to deal with – her dad a bully and her parents closing in on a breakup.

Upstairs, Laura navigated the mess of clothing, stuffed toys and books, on her bedroom floor. She flopped on the unmade bed and opened up her phone. On the bus home with Darlene, they'd wondered about Lyle's stormy exit from the lunchroom, but Darlene's texts had new light to throw.

"Cops picked up his mom. Guess fatgirl MaryLou told him."

"How you know?"

"Marylou's BFF Angie."

Any more news on the Lyle Prince front, Laura didn't need. The guy was already taking up too much room in her brain. Not once but twice today, Ms Lewis had given her a hard time for inattention in Math class. Lyle Prince, Laura kept telling herself, was a shitty little showoff, and what she especially hated was the way he'd made her sound like a fluttery airhead in the schoolyard. That was Mom, not her. Then she wished she hadn't thought that.

Laura wasn't ready for dating. Darlene and the others in their posse called her a single pringle. She favoured jeans over the leggings under don't-bend-over skirts the other girls wore. She knew she was a knockout and was not ungrateful for it, except for the times she saw it as a curse. Besides, she hadn't come across anyone worth a second look in the limited supply of young guys Southmead had to offer. Too many creeps, sniggering little groups in the schoolyard copping an eyeful when they thought she wasn't looking.

But why, oh why, couldn't she lose the image of Lyle standing by the counter in the Mini Mart, dark eyes burning in that lean, bony face, holding the gun on the two bozos? The memory raised an uncomfortable buzz.

Another text from Darlene:

Forget Lyle. Somethin else we got talk about. Like now. DQ 20 mins

Like what

DQ 20 mins

*

At Garth's place, five times that afternoon Lyle had called Mom. Her phone still didn't answer. A sneaky worry started and wouldn't be silenced. Where had Mom really gone yesterday after she'd dropped him off? To the store, she'd said, but had she? Garth should keep his dumb ideas to himself. He really wanted Mom to answer.

Garth's dad hadn't shown up yet, either. The event next door for Grandpa Millard was still going, presumably. Garth hadn't said much, sat and petted the dog, listened as Lyle made his calls. The three of them had restlessly watched some dumb influencer on YouTube to pass the time. No way was Lyle about to share his worries about Mom with Garth after the little nube had triggered them in the first place.

It would be dark soon. Go home, maybe get a ride from Monty or head for the Station and see if Mom was there? Garth had said his dad might help but he wasn't around. Lyle started pacing the family room. Garth stood too. "Hank's here, wanna see?"

"Say what?" Lyle raked his fingers through his hair. Had Garth said what he thought he had?

"They brought Hank Niles here last night. The roads were too bad to take him to the morgue in Kincardine. He's in the cooler. Be here till tomorrow prob'ly. Dad's cleaned him up a bit."

Lyle had never seen a dead body. Mom hadn't let him see Kenny when he died of Meningitis. Dead animals, plenty. People? No.

"So you up for taking a look?"

Garth's expression displayed mild curiosity. Lyle asked himself if this was some kind of dopey test. Come see the dead guy and don't freak out? One of those *Rights of passage* he'd heard people talk of?

Why not? Anything to take his mind off the anxiety roiling his brain. Lyle drew a long breath. "Sure, lead on."

Garth took him down the hall to the kitchen. Something on the stove smelled warm and meaty. Lyle wondered if he could snag an invite to supper. A door at the back gave onto a short, dark corridor with muffled sounds of the Millard visitation coming through the wall. At the far end they entered a cool white room that displayed medical-looking gear with tubes attached, two shiny white sinks and a dished metal table. Clear glass containers of various liquids stood on a shelf. A bright circular saw blade hung from the end of an articulated arm, now folded. It prompted disquieting images.

Garth beckoned. "Over here. Dad only has the two coolers, the accidents usually go straight to Kincardine for autopsy."

Yeah thanks Garth, could he skip the tour guide part? The room reeked of bleach like the indoor pool Dad used to take him to in Wingham. Had this been such a great idea? Too late, suck it up. Garth gripped the handle of a jumbo-size pantry drawer and slid it out a few feet.

There he was, Hank Niles, who Lyle had seen drive his fine old cars through town more times than he could count. Except it wasn't Hank. It might have been a wax statue like the ones in that place at Niagara Falls, except for a cheek sliced open and a dent in the side of the head above the left ear. But Hank Niles was not here.

So this was death, and it seemed somehow less momentous than Lyle had expected, less affecting. The waxy, utterly still thing before him was simply that, an object. Killing that rabbit had hit him harder than this. A poor suffering animal in a trap, and he'd seen it go. One minute alive, then dead. That was different.

Mom and Dad had not been churchgoers, or believers as far as he could tell, apart from a few muttered prayers when Kenny went to the hospital. Lyle didn't buy any of it. Jesus died to redeem our sins? Wasn't it kind of presumptuous to imply that everyone was a rotten sinner? And if God was such a great guy, all loving and all powerful, why did he let people get cancer, why did all the shitty things happen you'd see on the news every day, why did Kenny have to get a fever and then die? It was a scam. It made no sense and it didn't take a genius to see it.

And death? You died, period, end of story. Anything else was wishful thinking, fairytales.

Footsteps approached in the hallway.

6. RIDE IN THE HEARSE

Laura and Darlene sat at the Dairy Queen.

Laura's voice came out in a desperate whisper. "You did *what?* You told your Dad I know about the occupation? Dar, how could you do that?" Darlene clasped and unclasped her fingers. She wouldn't meet Laura's eyes. The Oreo Mini-Blizzard Cake stayed untouched.

"Stupid me, I messed up and he got a copy of the text, you know, the one I sent begging you to never ever tell." Darlene sniffed back tears, "and so he knows you know and I am so, so sorry."

Laura had the horrid sensation of things falling apart. First, the business with Lyle and the Mini Mart, then missing livestock and vandalism, now this. She had never thought about it before, but Southmead had always been a safe, secure place, boring beyond belief, but safe. No longer. She wished she could just go home and cuddle with her stuffies. Too bad she wasn't twelve anymore, nor ever would be again. Darleen was such a fool sometimes and this wasn't schoolyard gossip you could shrug off.

"What will I do, Dar? I'm not gonna tell anybody. Why would I?"

"That's what I told my dad, but he totally didn't like it. He went off muttering about how teenage girls could never keep secrets and how he'd look like a loose mouthed idiot and he couldn't risk it. I don't know, Laura. Some of these guys are really scary. Like, they carry guns." Darlene squeezed her eyes shut and tears ran down her cheeks.

*

Monty Priest, mouth set in exasperation, came through the door to the embalming room. "Garth, son, you absolutely can't be in here." Monty's face displayed more sorrow than anger. It was the face of a farmer, not a man who spent his days among the dead and bereaved, a face to which smiles would come easily because the world was full of positive energy and opportunity. Maybe that was the reason Mr Priest could handle the job he did.

"Come on you two," he said, "back in the house, now."

Lyle stared at the floor. "Yes, Mr Priest, sorry." No response from Garth, his face showing no hint of sorry.

Back in the kitchen, Lyle steeled himself for a Mom-style harangue but that wasn't Monty's way. Instead, he sat them down at the breakfast table and started to explain a few things.

"I need for you two to understand about respect for the dead." There was a gentle earnestness to his voice. "They aren't some exhibit for you to rubberneck at, and it doesn't matter if you think they went on to a better place or not, okay? The point is, they lived and they travelled life's path. They faced its good bits and its bad bits. And when it's over we owe them respect for the journey. Maybe if they were a very bad person, well, I guess not so much, but you see what I mean, guys? When we show respect for the dead we are actually respecting ourselves because, you know what? We're all headed down that road."

Monty had Lyle's full attention. No one had ever spoken to him about death this way, or at all.

"And when we have a visitation like the one for Grandpa Millard in there, it's to acknowledge *that*, celebrate their life as we like to say, and share memories, but, and this is something I've come to understand, it's solace for each other too, because, after all, nobody wants to be dead, do they? There was a poet, his name was Dylan Thomas, and he wrote a poem I call to mind at these moments. *Do not go gentle into that good night. Rage, rage against the dying of the light.*"

Shit yes, Lyle thought, I'd rage.

Garth looked like he'd heard this lecture before. "Dad, how are we supposed to respect every person who's died? That's way too many people." Monty opened his mouth to respond but his son spoke first.

"Dad, the cops picked up Lyle's Mom and she doesn't answer her phone. I told him you might know what to do. That's why he's here."

Monty's eyes widened. "When was this? My God Lyle, you should have told me sooner! Is this to do with the Mini Mart business?"

Garth answered. "He doesn't know. More likely it's about Mr Niles in there, if you ask me." He cocked his thumb and pointed over his shoulder toward the room with Hank and the circular saw.

"That's enough, son. Leave it now. Let's think about this." The thinking didn't take long. "Alright, first off, I'll call the station. I know the Chief pretty well, our jobs cross paths often enough."

Monty put the call on speakerphone. Nora the dispatcher answered. "Southmead Police, is this an emergency call?"

"No, Nora, it's Monty, is the Chief there for a quick word?"

"Not right now, Mr Priest. Can anyone else help you today?"

Lyle picked up on the formality. The call would be recorded.

"Nora, I need to track down Judy Prince. I have her son here with me and he heard she was picked up earlier by you folks. Naturally he's concerned. Can you tell me what this is about? Is it related to the Mini Mart business?"

"Mr Priest, you know I can't tell you what it's related to. The most I can say, and even this could get me in trouble, is it's not about the Mini Mart. Ms Prince got a ride home about twenty minutes ago. She'll be there by now, I'm sure."

Monty thanked the dispatcher and ended the call.

Lyle's sense of unease was turning closer to anger. He was in the clear, but Mom? What had she gone and done? Garth's off the wall theory didn't sound so off the wall anymore.

"Come on Lyle," Monty said, "I'll run you home in the hearse."

Lyle rolled his eyes. Whatever.

Monty wouldn't come in. "I'd best not, Lyle," he said with a shake of the head, "I don't think your mom would appreciate my company right now. You go on, and take it easy on her, okay?"

Mom had a carton of generic white wine open on the table. Lyle guessed she'd drunk half of it already. The ashtray was there too. Empty, but *that smell* hung in the air. Lyle had tried the stuff once. It made him want to puke.

They got into it. "How could they think I had anything to do with this?" Judy asked, her expression dull, her voice low. "Because I wrote Hank a nasty email? He deserved it, the SOB, after what he was trying to do to me."

Deserved what, the email or death? Could she really have done it? Go careful. "So, Mom, what did the cops ask you?"

"They wanted to know where I was between five and six yesterday afternoon. I told them how I took you home and then went back to the store.

'Course, they can't find anybody that saw me, can they? Not trying too hard I bet."

"How did they know you sent Hank an email in the first place?"

"Aw, c'mon Lyle. He passed it on to his big brother, didn't he? Wanted him to know what a bitch he had to deal with. Makes no difference though, does it? That's their big lead now. Didn't the idiot just run off the road in the storm? Oh no, that'd be way too easy. Let's have a murder investigation instead. Bastards. They have nothing, took my phone as well."

Lyle had to ask. "So it wasn't you then?"

Mom looked up. She seemed not to hear and took another slurp of wine. "Where have you been, anyway?"

Lyle's fingernails drummed on the tabletop. Anger and frustration were building, like when you were about to throw up and there was nothing you could do about it.

"What's it to you, Mom? Here you are with your stupid wine and your stupid smokes. What am I supposed to do? Tell me. You treat me like I'm some random kid who sorta hangs out here. Oh sure, that was a great display you put on at the station yesterday, but Mom, I gotta tell you, I don't think you give a shit where I've been."

Mom lowered her head, in her own bubble again, eyes glazed. They sat there for a minute, then she let out a sigh, took another hit of wine and looked up at her son.

"Won't it be great? Judy Prince, successful mother. You in the detention centre, because that's where you're headed, Lyle, I can see it, the other one in the cemetery, and now they think I did a murder and who have I got to stick up for me? Nobody, not one single damn person."

Lyle knew what was coming. He'd heard it too many times.

"Oh, Kenny. I thought it was the flu. How was I to know it was meningitis? And by the time your useless mother got her wits together and called an ambulance, you were too far gone." The tears streamed down Judy's face, and Lyle, as usual, had no response. Kenny, the big brother who got things right. Lyle remembered the final winter, the two of them and Garth with a hockey-net on the backyard rink, lit by re-purposed Christmas lights like the picture on a lame Christmas card.

And then Kenny wasn't around anymore, and that was the problem. Mom had never said, but Lyle knew, in the place where he buried uncomfortable truths, that once Kenny had gone he was expected to step up. He'd tried, in his way. He'd worked at becoming the schoolyard tough guy, the one the other kids accorded grudging respect. And so they did, or maybe only pretended to? But it was wearing thin, this act, because he still felt like the kid brother inside, the one who could never get anything totally right, the one who would never, despite the boasting and the bravado, get close to anyone like the amazing Laura. Attitude might be getting old.

But what was he supposed to do? Mom sat there zoned out. Nobody to help, she'd said. Should he get up and give her a hug? He didn't feel like it. And this scary Hank business. He wouldn't have the first notion about where to start. Did he even care? Because there were times when the woman sitting across the table seemed, not a stranger of course, far from it, more like somebody he knew all too well and would cross the street to avoid.

*

Lyle raided the fridge for the remains of yesterday's pizza, zapped it and took it to his room. What Monty'd said about respect had stayed with him. How respect for those no longer here was respecting yourself too. In a corner, half hidden under a pile of clothes, was a cardboard carton. Lyle took a bite of pizza, shoved the clothes on the floor and pulled the carton over by his bed. He sat and contemplated it. He didn't perform this ritual too often and was on the point of skipping it now. Then he recalled Monty's words, what they meant. He reached in. DVDs, *Band of Brothers* the boxed set, comics, a Redwings Jersey, a scarred puck. Kenny's stuff.

Whenever he did this, it felt utterly strange, though it wasn't as if Kenny's spirit was there or anything gay like that. But even so, Lyle hung suspended in the grip of forces he had no clue about.

And memories would surface. Not too long ago, life had been fun. Summer trips to the beach when it never rained, and the hotdogs were always delicious. Mom and Dad laughing and horsing around. Schoolyard games and no bullying. Kenny mostly protective, never too rough when they had play fights. Mom there to greet him when the bus dropped him off.

All gone, those untroubled times. Dad behind bars, Kenny dead, no more trips to the beach, the life Lyle remembered all smashed and broken.

But what was it he'd told Garth? "Friends gotta stick by each other?" He didn't remember ever saying or thinking this before, but as he sat there on his bed, holding Kenny's hockey jersey, it occurred to Lyle that perhaps the same thing applied to families, even to what was left of his.

Maybe Mom could use some company after all. He slumped downstairs to watch TV until bedtime, fetched a bowl of chips for himself and one for her.

7. CHICKEN CHARLIE

An insistent hammering noise. In his half-dream, Lyle pictured Hank Niles, fists thumping on the walls of the drawer, alive after all like a zombie. He jolted awake, bathed in sweat despite the cold in his room, the result of Mom turning down the baseboard heaters at night to save on the Hydro.

Lyle rolled out of bed and checked the clock: 6am. Would the cops come after Mom this early? He pulled on a hoodie over his pyjama shorts and nearly collided with his mother on her way to the front door.

"Go away!" she yelled, "I'm calling 911 right now, so you better get lost, whoever you are!"

A man's voice answered. "Ms Prince, it's the McDonalds, Laura's parents. We need to talk to you, can we come in?"

Judy opened the door a crack against the security chain "Why are you here, waking us up this time of the morning?"

Lyle nudged her, "Mom, let them in, alright? They'll freeze their butts off out there."

Judy popped the chain, opened the door and stepped back. The McDonalds entered with a gust of freezing air and Judy closed the door in a hurry. She turned without a word and went to stand by her chair. "So what is it?"

Laura's mom pushed back her hood. Her hair, red-gold like her daughter's, was matted on her forehead. She was distraught, eyes wild. Lyle had a feeling about what was coming.

"Is my daughter here? We don't know here she is and all we hear now is, *Lyle this, and Lyle that.*" Dr McDonald touched his wife's shoulder as if to calm her, but to no effect. "Laura," she called out, "are you here my darling?"

Judy threw her hands wide. "What kind of people do you think we are? Taken off, has she? Why the hell would you think she was here?"

Dr MacDonald's face bore deep creases of strain and worry. "I'm sorry, but Lyle, I have to ask, do you have any idea where she might be?"

Lyle shook his head.

"You see, we heard sounds in the night, a car in our driveway. I came down and looked outside and there was a note taped to the door. It was from Laura and it said she was fine, had gone away for a few days, and not to call the police. Her phone's not answering. We don't know what to think. She's never done anything like this."

"Are you sure the note was from her?" Lyle asked.

Laura's mom brought a fist to her mouth. "Oh please don't say that! What if somebody made her write it? Oh God, what if somebody has her!"

Cold fingers of dread clenched in Lyle's chest. Not for the first time, the memory of Bigelow's warning surfaced. Could he and his mate have been that stupid? Visions of Laura in the hands of those two dirtbags arose and wouldn't be shoved aside. Those two *could* be that stupid.

Judy spoke up, her sense of outrage thankfully under control. "You have to tell the police. You can't *not*. Look, you said there was a car, so somebody else is involved, right? Show the police the note, see what they make of it. Oh my goodness, I can't imagine what you're going through! I almost wish Laura *had* been here for you." Judy stepped over to Ms MacDonald, who was weeping quietly, and put an arm around her shoulder. Compassion was an emotion Lyle hadn't seen in his Mom since forever.

But now here came that same sense of futility from yesterday, the inability to make a difference. Had Laura simply run away of her own accord? What if she hadn't? How would anyone go about finding her? And what had Laura's mother said? *All we hear about is Lyle?* What? He was on her mind after all? Enough already, Lyle shook his head in bafflement. Too many dumb questions and the futility was getting to him. He had to do something. Anything.

*

Billy Niles was up early that morning as well. "Gotta go see Charlie Webb," he whispered to his barely awake wife. He showered and dressed. The Beemer waited sleek and silvery in the heated triple-car garage. The driveway, lined with Balsam firs, was nicely ploughed and the wrought-iron gates slid open at a touch of the remote. Billy drove through town, hit the drive-thru for a Dark

Roast and a breakfast bagel — sausage, no bacon — and headed south. Ten minutes down the road he took a left down highway eighteen.

No weather today, a nondescript day, grey skies. The sandwich sat like a lard brick in his gut. He was feeling the tension. That reporter woman still around, Hank's funeral to arrange, a Co-op board meeting — could he put it off on compassionate grounds? — and, before he even got to next week, the occupation. Was the whole scheme going to work? Please let it not have been a disastrous mistake.

Billy was finding it hard to take a breath, could feel a pulse in his neck and wondered if he was having a panic attack. Then it passed. Too late now for second thoughts, like he'd told Hank. He would miss Hank. It hadn't been brotherly love exactly, and they'd disagreed over many things, but still, he never should have died that way. Judy Prince — there was history there and that email. He'd bet she'd had a hand in it and she would pay. The properties on Main Street were his now and kicking her out would be sweet.

Five miles down the road, two long, low sheds, originally black, now peeling and patchy, came into view. Between them and the road lay a jumble of outbuildings. Billy remembered the stink from the sheds. It could make a person retch. Chicken Charlie Webb had two hundred hens incarcerated in there, in cages barely big enough to keep them alive and popping out the product. Billy got a stomach-turning whiff as he waited for Charlie to answer the door of his dilapidated bungalow.

Inside, the smell changed to cooking grease and cigarettes. Billy declined Charlie's chicken-poop-perfumed coffee and stayed with the remains of his dark roast. Charlie launched into his predictable rant. "Convert to free-range, they say. Who are we kidding here? Three times the floorspace and double the labour costs. Can I get a government subsidy? Could I pass the costs along to the processors? Gimme a break! Are we supposed to sit here on our asses and get our livelihoods taken? No goddamn way, my friend. Time for a demonstration."

Billy gave a grim half-smile. Ever since a gang of libertarian throwbacks had occupied the headquarters of a National Wildlife Refuge in Oregon, talk had gone around a certain faction within the Co-op about staging an occupation of their own. Billy had seen an opportunity and encouraged the group for reasons far removed from anything the would-be occupiers could have suspected.

Charlie was barely getting started. "The family farms are closing, gettin' bought out by conglomerates or some asshole hedge fund that wants to dig a godforsaken huge quarry. The dairy farmers are the only ones makin' any money. You checked the price of cheese lately? Eh?" Charlie's head nodded like a tacky rear-window ornament. "What about the rest of us? Eh? Government keeps cuttin' these trade deals and the labour's headed for the cities."

Billy nodded sagely. He'd heard it all so many times. Let the fool rave on. This was the whole point of the visit, a final stir of the pot, make sure everything was a go.

"Charlie, you know I admire and support you one hundred percent," he said. "I've tried my best and we've had some small successes but your brave initiative is going to wake up the politicians and get the public on our side. The press will eat it up, especially *The Beacon*. And I'll be there for you when it goes down. That's why I have to deny all foreknowledge, and I know you get that." He sure hoped Charlie got it.

Charlie's face went from agitated to solemn. "Very sorry to hear about Hank. I guess I was one of the last to see him. He didn't agree with the occupation, he made it only too clear the night he died, but still. When will they lay him to rest?"

"It has to be after Monday because of the timing. I have to talk to Monty Priest. Let you know."

It was time for more immediate business, and then out of here. "So did Mitch do a run yesterday?"

"Yup, sure did. But I think he wants a bigger slice. Kept on about the risk. He thinks Jacob Ryan wants a piece of him."

"Thanks Charlie, for letting me know. I'll see to Mitch. So?"

Charlie grinned a thin grin. "Oh, yeah." He got up, walked to a cupboard and came back with a black garbage bag. "It's all here as far as I know, but count it if you want."

"Just the envelopes, counted in your presence if you get my drift, 'case of any issues with Mitch."

Charlie gave Billy a sideways glance and nodded. "Smart move, Bill, for both of us if you know what I mean." He upended the bag and a pile of brown envelopes slid out. Billy counted, Charlie observed.

"I make that fourteen." Billy said.

Charlie gave a thumbs-up. "Fourteen confirmed. Had a busy day, didn't he?"

"He sure did. That's fourteen permits I gotta get off to the Ministry toot sweet. All in a day's work. So Charlie, here you go." Niles reached into his jacket and produced an envelope, brown like the ones from the bag but a lot smaller. He passed it over and the two shook. Niles used the politician's favourite move as seen on TV news, left hand gripping Charlie's right shoulder, he'd never been much for hugging men. Still, one last push of encouragement wouldn't hurt.

"All the best for tomorrow, my friend," he said. "Are the guys from Huron County still in, and Northumberland?"

"Them and more besides," answered Chicken Charlie, "the response has been great, really great. We got militia guys coming all the way from Madoc."

"Fantastic, Charlie," Billy replied, his voice low and earnest, "there's gonna be headlines across the country. You'll be making history." As if deprived of speech by the depth of his emotions, he turned, picked up the garbage bag of donations, and made for the door. The reek from the barns caught his throat well before he'd made it to the Beemer.

The Madoc Militia? Jesus Christ! That hadn't been part of the plan. Those fuckheads came armed, thought the world needed fixing and they'd be the ones to do it. Billy felt the panic attack returning but he managed to quell the flutters in his chest. Militias? Nothing to be done about it now. What have you done Charlie, you damn fool?

8. DOGS UNDERSTAND

It was driving Lyle crazy. What could be happening to Laura right this moment? He had to talk to somebody, anybody, and there weren't many choices.

After a 6am wakeup, early for him, a ride downtown with Mom on her way to work beat hanging around the house and dropping in on Garth at weekends was established practice. In summer they'd snag a ride over to Lee's place to look at motorbikes or strike out into what Garth termed *The so-called countryside* to annoy the livestock. In wintertime, video games mostly. Today was hardly a normal Saturday though. Mom under suspicion, Laura gone missing.

Mom got her usual at the drive-thru, Lyle, a donut and a hot chocolate. Neither of them was much for conversation but Mom did express concern and sympathy for Laura's parents.

"They have to call the police. They can't just sit around waiting and hoping for her to show up, can they? Can you imagine what that would be like? I'd call if you went missing, that's for sure."

Lyle had no answer, so he grunted and munched on his donut. On top of the scary worries about Laura and Mom, the last forty-eight hours had left him with uneasy insights about families and…stuff. Like seeing the 3D version of a movie after you'd watched the regular one.

He wouldn't really have crossed the street to avoid Mom, he'd only thought that because she was always yapping on at him. She was his mother after all. That was the way life worked. Nobody ever told you this, you had to figure it out. Most likely some people never did.

Laura, he said to himself, what on earth are you up to? How could you do this to your parents? If she'd taken off of her own accord then she was going to get the mother of all bawling-outs and not only from them, from him too, whether she despised him or not. But she must know that, mustn't she? Then why? Something must have spooked her that she'd go and run away like that.

Or was her disappearance something far worse, too awful to think about? Because if it was, then somebody better get on the case, like now. Would Chief Harrington and his band of clowns take it seriously? Nah. They'd think, Oh, a silly teenager having a crisis, back in a few days for sure, no reason to go off the deep end.

Mom dropped Lyle off at Sunset Vistas and Garth greeted him with the kind of line Lyle simply couldn't get his head around. "Dad's out back embalming." Lyle pictured Monty practising his dark arts with the saw and those liquids from the shelf. Strictly off-limits and that was perfectly fine, thanks. "But he knew you'd be here and he said he has a surprise for you, so stick around. He'll be done in a bit. He got me a new video game, come check it out."

Lyle decided to keep the news about Laura to himself until Monty showed up. Telling the whole thing twice would be too much.

Garth's access to video games was under the strict control of his father. No *Carmaggedon* or *Soldier of Fortune* hereabouts. Usually some wimpy shit like *Pokemon*. The pair flopped down in the high-ceilinged family room, its walls hung with framed citations and thank-you letters from clients of the funeral home.

Garth fired up the X-Box. "Check this out." *Brothers* turned out to be visually amazing and it did halfway take Lyle's mind off things. Two brothers had to collaborate, solve problems and make it to a final goal. Not much violence, but death was always in the background. At one point they had to cross a battlefield strewn with corpses. That felt appropriate, here at good ol' Sunset Vistas.

Ranger showed up for companionship and the possibility of treats. Monty was still not to be seen. The dog got a treat but wouldn't settle and made his wishes clear by pawing at the door. Garth paused the game. "He needs to defecate. You coming?" Quite the privilege, being invited to take Ranger for a crap. Lyle had immersed himself in *Brothers* but Garth had the master controller, so he had no choice. Garth went to let his dad know they were walking Ranger.

Lyle pulled on his parka and boots. He opened conversation with the dog. "So Ranger buddy, what's up?" Ranger ceased pawing at the door and sat. He looked up at Lyle with the sincere and concerned gaze only dogs seemed able to summon. Could they tell what you were thinking, feeling? You bet they could. Lyle reached down and scratched the dog's ears. Ranger placed his head against Lyle's leg and it felt like Ranger told him, "We dogs understand. We've been hanging out with you humans forever. When we hunted together, the guys who kept their cool were the ones who brought home dinner. Be calm, Lyle, be smart. You can handle this. Be a hunter."

Equipped with the obligatory plastic bag, the trio hit Main Street. They came up on the Mini Mart and passed by without comment. Then Ranger decided to do the pre-business doggy dance. Saturday morning was the busiest Southmead ever got in Winter, but nobody took notice when Ranger took a dump right there on the sidewalk.

Except: "Hey, buddy, go ahead and let your dog do it where people have to step, why don't you?"

You couldn't mistake that voice. He turned and Marigold Wallace, winsome young reporter, stood before him, hands on hips. Recognition dawned and she looked borderline embarrassed. "Oh, hi Lyle, how are you? Look, I mean, does your friend have to let him go right there? It's kind of disgusting, you know?"

Those sincere brown eyes — no giant sunglasses today — carried a challenge that had him stumbling for a reply.

"Uh, hi, Ms Wallace. No, see, it's the snowbanks. He'd have to climb over and do it in the traffic. So it's kind of accepted round here. In the wintertime, right Garth? This is my friend Garth. And this is Ranger."

Garth nodded and stooped to retrieve the dog's steaming offering. Lyle had to smirk as Ranger, no doubt sensing possible discord, sat before Marigold and gave her a canine grin with major eye-contact. It worked. Marigold reached out and rubbed his head.

"Pleased to meet you Ranger. I guess you gotta do what you gotta do, boy." She smiled and adjusted the plaid scarf which nicely set off her red ski-jacket. "So Lyle, I haven't heard from you. Thought you were going to be my eyes and ears about the weird stuff around here. You still got my card?"

Lyle nodded. "Sorry Ms Wallace. I got kind of sidetracked." He explained to Garth about Marigold and her mission here in Southmead. "So, Garth, do you wanna tell her?"

Garth rose to the occasion and managed to give a coherent account of the tire slashing on his street. He insisted on including the missing cat story as well, despite Lyle's throat-clearing.

"Thanks guys, this helps but, like I said, my editor's getting impatient. I'm up for a promotion to Senior Reporter and I need a story. Keep your ears open, okay?"

Lyle came to a decision. "Garth, why don't you head back? I need to speak to this lady, just the two of us, you know? Personal stuff. Catch up with you back at your place. We'll restart the game where you paused it, okay?"

Garth rolled his shoulders and looked from one to the other. "No Lyle, you gotta head back with me. Dad's got a surprise for you, remember?"

"Garth, I'll only be a minute, promise."

Garth started shaking his head back and forth, a sure sign of stress. Lyle put an arm across his shoulder. "It's okay, buddy, I'll be there pronto, I won't let you down."

"Whatever. Goodbye then, Ms Wallace. Lyle, you gotta be there by eleven."

"Goodbye Garth," Marigold said, "you too Ranger. Nice meeting you both and thanks for the update. Here's my card if you hear anything more." Garth accepted the card and wandered off, still shaking his head and muttering to himself, bag of poo in one hand, dog's leash in the other.

It had dawned on Lyle that he had tradable information, and he needed to trade it with somebody in the know, somebody who could find stuff out. Standing right there in front of him, radiating curiosity, was such a person.

Marigold, he judged, would appreciate a direct approach, "So, you're looking for a story, right? Well, I sure have one for you but I need help too. Can we deal?"

"What kind of help?"

"Information. The kind you might be able to get. It's about the story I have, two stories in fact. And both of them make a few slashed tires look like nothing."

Marigold looked sceptical, the corners of her mouth turned down, acting the hard-nosed newspaperwoman not about to be fooled by this kid from a hick town.

"Why do you want information?" She asked.

"People I care about are involved."

"What sort of stories?"

"Wait a minute. If I tell you, I want something back. Especially to know what the cops are thinking. That's what you reporters are good at, right?"

Marigold shook her head. "Lyle Prince, you watch too much TV. The cops in these small towns won't tell a reporter the damn weather forecast. But look here, if your stories are worth following, then okay, I will promise to let you know anything I find that could help. But now it's your turn, sir. What d'ya got?"

"There was a road accident the day before yesterday. Guy drove off the road in the snowstorm and got himself killed."

"That's old news. I already did a couple of paragraphs for the paper. What's your other story?"

A snowplough approached, its blade grinding and clanking on the road. Lyle waited for it to pass. "Hold on, if you're such a great reporter, how come you don't know the cops are looking into it, like maybe it wasn't an accident? And my other story? A teenage girl went missing last night, Laura MacDonald. Remember her from the courtroom? I don't think the cops know about it yet, so there's a scoop for you. You interested now? Which story do you want to hear first?"

Marigold was interested alright. Her big eyes gleamed with excitement.

"Let's get out of the cold," she said, "come on, I'll buy you a milkshake or something across the street." They turned to climb the snowbank. Lyle offered a hand and Marigold took it. She didn't object when he held on until they'd navigated the other small mountain on the far side.

Inside the Dairy Queen, Marigold got Lyle his favourite Chocolate Banana Smoothie and a black coffee for herself. They found a corner at the back and he told his stories.

Marigold finished scribbling in her notebook. "Wow," she said, "you sure kept your side of the deal. Now I have to figure out how to keep mine. But this little arrangement has to be strictly between us. You get it? No exceptions, not your mom, not Garth, not anybody."

"I get it."

"So give me your number."

There being no alternative, Lyle reeled off the Prince home number.

They parted company and as he watched Marigold head off down the street, Lyle experienced a tingle of excitement. Was it thanks to time spent in the attentive company of a cute woman? Yeah, but not entirely, because it occurred to him that in making his deal with Marigold he'd followed Ranger's advice to keep his cool. The anxiety wasn't going anywhere but he'd finally started, as best he could, to do something about it.

9. INFORMATION

Back at Garth's, "You took your time with that lady," Garth said. Lyle always knew when Garth was put out. His features became even more impassive and his voice went all quiet so you had to strain to hear.

"Sorry, buddy. When your dad gets back I'll tell you the whole story, and then you'll understand, promise."

"Dad's back already. He's in his office. He gave me a hard time when I returned without you, said you'd better be here by eleven. You only just made it. Come on."

Lyle barely got time to wonder about the reason for the urgency. Garth ushered him down the familiar dark corridor, past the cold storage and embalming room, and, without knocking, shoved him through the door to Monty's office. Monty turned from the window, phone in hand. He spoke into it. "He's here, give me one second."

Monty paused and sighed. "Lyle, I've interfered and taken liberties. You can be mad at me if you want, but on the other end of this phone is your dad. I've told him about what's going on with your mom. He wants to talk to you."

A swirl of emotions and memories. The long-gone trips to the beach, the utter dismay of Dad being carted off to jail, Mom screaming at the cops. Those images would never, ever, go away and he was forced to relive them every time they spoke, which was no more often than every couple of months. Monty moved to the door. "Come on, Son," he said to Garth, "we'll give Lyle some privacy."

Lyle sensed this call was going to be different. He took the handset. "Dad?"

His father's warm baritone sounded over the connection. "Hey, kid, first thing, don't forget to give Monty a big thank-you for this. He had to call in favours to set it up."

Lyle wondered what kind of favours from a funeral director in Southmead could induce the flinty officers at Maplehurst prison to grant a phone call at short notice. "Sure Dad, you doin' okay?" A break with tradition right there.

"Same-same. I can look after myself. Even started a computer course, can you believe that? But hey, we don't have time for small talk. What's going on with your mother? Monty only told me the cops are looking at her about Hank Niles. Do you know any more? How's she holding up?"

Lyle didn't get this. The same puzzled annoyance came over him like he'd felt at Mom last night. "Dad, why aren't you asking her instead of me?"

"Son, when Monty set this call up he told me your Mom doesn't want my input right now, so there it is. What the hell is happening up there?"

"Dad, all I know is, Mom sent Hank an email, and he took it as a threat and now the cops have it. The evening it happened she left me home to go to the store, but she said nobody's come forward to confirm she was there."

"Ah Jesus, what a goddamn mess. An email huh? That's kind of thin. Wait a minute, Hank was dead, so how'd the cops get it?"

"I dunno how they got it, they aren't gonna say, are they? Mom figured Hank must have showed it to his brother before the accident and then Billy gave it to the cops, or maybe they found it on Hank's computer? If they're even that smart, which I doubt. But Dad, Billy Niles really doesn't like our family, you know? When we were in court on Wednesday, you could tell. So anyway…"

"Back up, back up! What's this about court?"

Ah jeez, Dad didn't know about the Mini Mart caper.

"Dad, I was in the Mini Mart when two clowns busted in and tried to pull a holdup. Then Wowchuk came in and arrested them. But I had to go to court and tell what I saw. It was no big deal but Niles showed up to bail these guys out. Too much happening Dad, you know?"

"Billy Niles. Well, imagine that. Here you are, Mom in trouble, probably 'cos Niles passed on some bullshit email, and look who bails out two guys who obviously hate your guts? Niles again."

Dad paused. "Son, it's time you knew this. Guess who was behind the case that got me in here? No prize for guessing. Mister Billy Niles, the biggest extortion artist and sleaze-bag in the county. He gets what he calls donations from farmers in return for production permits."

Something went click in Lyle's head. "Dad, I'm fourteen, you're right, tell me, 'cos things up here are getting kind of weird."

"Lyle, I don't need to burden you with all the details. What's done is done."

"Dad, like I said, I'm not a little kid anymore. You want me to be there for Mom? I need to know the whole story."

He heard a sigh.

"So your mother never told you much?"

"Nothing."

"Well, I wasn't making a lot of money with casual work. Drive somebody's tractor, run a bailer. Best job I ever had was driving a backhoe for Wally Nesbit, clearing ditches mostly. It was steady work, but only for three seasons. So, long story short, I fell in with the wrong crowd. We did jobs for somebody we never met and who's name we didn't know. There was this one individual, called himself Rufe, not his real name for sure. And there was a place out on Number Eight Sideroad, this old barn with a workshop. I remember it had a couple of Jesus-big silos by the turn in. And there was a tunnel underneath. It went down to the ravine, used to be for bootlegging, Rufe told us. Anyway, a couple of us would get the word to show up when Rufe had a project for us. That's what he called them. He would have the thing scoped out and he'd tell us where."

This was fascinating. Lyle willed Dad to keep going.

"It was farm equipment mostly, backhoes, tractors, mowers, ATVs sometimes. Two of us would go, after midnight always. We'd winch the thing on a flatbed and hightail it to the barn. That was the dicey part. Once it was there we'd strip the plates and VIN numbers. Then some guy would show up with a van, off he'd go with it, and we'd get paid and head out. It was a stupid way to make a buck, Lyle. There were a dozen chances to get busted. Surveillance cameras, alarms, who knows what.

"So of course one night on the way to the barn, here I am with a Kubota on the flatbed. Officer Jensen shows up flashing his lights behind me. The other guy was ahead of me in his truck and he took off. I don't blame him."

Lyle broke in, "Dad, wait a minute. Aren't you in there for armed robbery?"

Dad gave a bitter laugh. "Told you I was stupid, didn't I? Had my piece under the seat. They found it o'course, so it took all of five seconds for them to call it armed robbery, and here I am."

"Yeah Dad, but where does Billy Niles come into it?"

A long pause. Another sigh. Lyle heard a hard voice in the background ripping somebody up and down for some petty violation of prison rules.

"Kid, I didn't plan on telling this part but I guess I have to. Hank Niles and your mother were an item once upon a time. This was before I showed up. But every so often, even after we were together, he'd try and contact her. Behaving like he had some claim on her, the...never mind. So, this particular time she told me about it and I warned him off. Like really warned him off, know what I mean?"

"And wouldn't you know it, the very next week I got busted, and that, my friend, was no coincidence. Jensen wasn't out there in the middle of nowhere by accident. I could never prove it but I learned some stuff in here and, trust me, he was tipped off. And based on what I heard, Mr Goddamn Billy Niles was the one who did it."

Something didn't add up with Dad's story.

"But Dad, if Niles was the boss of the thieving scheme, why would he risk it all like that?"

"No, no, I'm not saying he was the boss guy, but one of his little helpers was the spotter, Mitch Bigelow. He'd go round the farms collecting permit money for Niles, and he'd see a nice tractor or whatever, sitting unprotected, and pass the word. So, who was better placed to make the anonymous call to the cops, and who had a better reason? Nobody I know of. So there you go. Bottom line? Billy put me in here."

Mitch Bigelow again. But no, Dad had put himself in there, the dumb-ass. Still, Lyle pictured Niles in court baling out the two losers, Brad Watts and, yes folks, give it up for asshole number one, Mitch Bigelow.

He decided to change the channel. "Dad, who would want to kill Hank Niles?"

"So you think he was killed, not an accident?"

"Well, Harrington and his crew think so, don't they?"

"Yeah, but..."

"Dad, how would somebody have done it, anyway?"

"Messed with his car maybe, the brakes. But right before he hit the hill? I dunno, sounds like a stretch, to anybody but the cops that is. Those jackasses'll build a case on nothing. Wait a minute! Potter's hill's on the way back to town from that barn. Why the hell else would Hank be cruising around in a snowstorm out there?"

Came the hard voice from before, "Time's up, Prince, say your goodbyes, make it snappy."

"One last thing, Son. Watch yourself. Don't go nosing around, okay? There's some bad dudes still kickin' around up there. Two of Rufe's crew were getting on the wrong side of him and then one day they weren't around anymore. So stay away, you hear me?"

Art's voice bore regret of a man who knew he had messed up. "Gotta go, kid, take care and say hi to Mom. Tell her I love her."

"Bye Dad."

Mr Billy Niles. Hank at the barn right before his fatal accident. Lyle was beginning to get a sense of things connecting, but he hadn't put it together yet. Right now he needed to keep his promise to tell Garth and Monty about Laura.

Back in the family room, Lyle described the McDonalds' early morning visit, the note on their door, the sound of a vehicle in the night, all of it.

Monty shook his head, dismayed. "My God Lyle, this is awful. First your mom and now this. Do you know if Laura's parents talked to the police?"

Lyle didn't know.

"Can you find out?"

"Maybe." Lyle wasn't ready to reveal his deal with Marigold. Would it even amount to anything? She could be playing him.

Garth, who had remained quiet, got up from where he'd been sitting with Ranger. He looked ready to say something.

"Think about it. Nothing ever happens here and then, all of a sudden what have we got? A guy killed, a girl disappearing, tires getting slashed, pets missing? Obviously it's all connected. Something's going to happen Dad, can't you see it?"

Monty gave his son a sceptical smile, but after the way Garth had predicted the cops' interest in Mom, Lyle wasn't so inclined to dismiss his theories. Did Laura know something she wasn't supposed to? Was that why she was missing? Voluntarily or, please no, otherwise?

Monty paced the room. "Lyle, I want to help. I wish I could think how."

Garth spoke up. "Dad, he badly needs a phone. Where's the one you had before you got the iPhone?"

"Let me go see." Monty left the room. Lyle shook his head. "Garth, it's the payment plan's the problem. We can't afford it."

Garth regarded his friend, expressionless. "Wait, will you?"

Monty reappeared with a phone and a charger, the phone black plastic, nothing fancy.

Garth spoke up. "He's worried about the cost of the plan, Dad. Tell him."

"No plan with this one, it's prepaid. You go online and buy minutes, enough to last a few months maybe. This one has a good few left on it. So give it a try. When the minutes get low, I'll help out, okay?"

This was excellent. Lyle knew he was one of the few kids who didn't have a phone. People at school knew it too. Somebody would ask for his number so they could text him and he would mumble something about his phone being broken. But they knew.

He did his best to graciously thank Monty, who put an arm around his shoulder and told him, "My pleasure, Lyle. Think this will help you?"

"Sure, me'n Garth can stay connected. It'll be great!"

Monty shook his head. "No, I mean how will it help you with your mom's problem? And Laura? Wasn't that the whole point here? Or did I misunderstand?"

Lyle' cheeks got hot. He knew he'd screwed up but the excitement of finally having a phone had eclipsed his worries for a brief moment.

"No, Mr Priest, I wasn't thinking. I guess getting a phone's pretty special when everybody else has one and you don't."

"Fair enough Lyle, but I'll only say this once. Your mom and I have known each other a long time. She's a good woman. You're all she's got — she'd cut off her right arm for you. Don't you know that? Do your best to be there for her. Family looks after family, Lyle. Here endeth the sermon." Monty looked embarrassed, like maybe he'd overstepped again.

Lyle remembered sitting on his bed holding Kenny's hockey jersey. "Okay Mr Priest, no problem. Thanks for the reminder." He gazed at the phone. It sat there in his hand, challenging him to get busy and operate it like a normal teenager. Monty's own phone chimed and he stepped into the hallway to take the call.

"You're clueless about that thing, aren't you? Wanna lesson?" Garth had his own phone out and was jabbing at it.

Lyle's new toy chimed and vibrated.

"I just texted you, so here's what you do."

It didn't take long to get a handle on the basics. Garth was a whiz at Twitter and Snapchat and Instagram, the little showoff, but those could come later, and the keyboard was so frickin' small. But Lyle had joined the ranks of the connected and it felt darn good. Garth showed him how to set up his contacts, Mom, and Garth himself of course. When he added Marigold Garth raised his eyebrows but kept quiet. There was one more number Lyle badly wanted: Laura's. He was pretty sure her parents wouldn't give it out but he really had to get that number. He hadn't figured out how yet, but he would.

10. DON'T MESS WITH A FREIGHT TRAIN

Saturday afternoon became a wheel-spinning chapter of indecision and speculation. Video games, another walk with Ranger, and more video games, none of it helped. Had Laura really run away like her note said? Why would she, had she done it before? Her parents said not. He had to get her number.

And then there was Hank's death. Had the cops found evidence of his car being messed with? Mom ought to get a lawyer but there was no way she had that kind of money. The talk went in circles and when Monty offered him a ride home for the second night running, Lyle accepted, mentally exhausted.

Back home, Mom had her carton of wine on the side table again.

"Leach came by," she said, "he brought back my phone, and a typical dumb warning not to leave town. Sure, like where am I gonna go? Take off to my villa in Palm Beach? Ha!"

"Hey Mom, I got a phone now too."

Her eyes narrowed. "Show me."

Lyle displayed his prized acquisition. Mom opened her mouth. "Now where did...?" Lyle knew she was remembering the only other time he'd had a phone, the one he'd ripped off out of Sally Barnes' backpack. He'd not understood how fast a phone could be traced. The same day, a cop car pulled up outside. Mom managed to talk them into letting it go as a kid's prank. Embarrassing hardly covered it.

Lyle cut her off. "Mom, chill out. Mr Priest gave it to me. Check with him if you don't believe me. And before you ask, it's got minutes on it and Mr Priest said he'll get me some more when it runs out."

Relief showed on Mom's face. "Did you tell him about my problem with the cops?"

"Yes, and he thought it would be good for me to have a phone, you know, seeing as you're under suspicion and all."

"Monty is a good man. Sometimes I wonder...well, I hope you thanked him properly."

"I did."

"Alright, supper's in half an hour. Your room is a mess. Go tidy it and bring out your laundry."

"Uh, Mom, there's something else."

"Lyle, quit with the excuses. Go tidy your room like I asked you."

Fine, if she didn't want to hear about the call with Dad, too bad. Lyle pushed past his mother and went to his room.

He had no intention of tidying. Other priorities. Do the easy one first, call Marigold and give her the number of his new phone. She answered right away, sounds of a busy bar or restaurant in the background.

"Oh hi, Lyle, nothing for you yet, maybe tomorrow." Lyle explained how he simply wanted to pass along his new contact number, so it was a short call, Marigold sounding preoccupied. She had a date, didn't she? Hey, if it kept her in Southmead, fine, good, but a twinge of jealousy came and went.

Now the tough one. Get Laura's number. Would her parents give it out? Asking them would be a last resort and he'd probably get the brushoff anyway. Nah, Darlene would be a better bet, and if she was such big buddies with Laura, maybe she'd know something.

There couldn't be too many Falconers in Southmead. Lyle reached across to the table that served as his homework desk and grabbed the crappy cheap laptop the school gave out — most of the kids had their own MacBooks. The White Pages listed two Falconers. Lyle didn't want Mom hearing this call so he decided to burn some minutes. He tried the first number, an address on 9th Concession. An elderly female voice answered.

Lyle did his best to adopt a respectful telephone manner. "Hello, I'm trying to contact Darlene Falconer, do I have the right number?"

"Oh no, young man, I'm her grandmother. They live over on the Brookfield road."

The woman refused to confirm the other number. Most likely thought he was some horny kid after Darlene, so Lyle apologized for the inconvenience and said goodbye.

A gruff male voice answered on the Brookfield Road number.

"Yeah?"

Lyle again sensed a need to be smooth. "Oh, hi. Mr Falconer? My name is Lyle Prince. I go to Southmead High with Darlene. I was hoping to speak to her."

"Lyle Prince, I know you. Where d'you get this number?"

"Uh, sir, it's in the phone book."

"Bullshit, they don't give out phone books anymore. Try again."

The voice was laced with rude resentment. Lyle had heard all about Darlene's dad.

"Sir, I meant the phone book on the internet, not like the actual *book*."

"Goddammit, where did our privacy go? Damn government knows everything about us. One of these days it's all gonna blow up, I'm telling you."

Lyle couldn't think of a suitable answer, so he kept quiet.

"What do you want with my daughter anyway?"

"Oh, we've got this geography assignment, and well, I gotta be honest, it's not my best subject. I need a bit of help."

"Sorry kid, you're out of luck."

Sure the guy was sorry, Lyle could hear the gloating.

"She's got Volleyball practice, gone with her mother. Can't help ya." Darlene's father hung up.

Lyle couldn't bear to wait on this any longer. During the phone calls, horrid visions of what might be happening to Laura kept surfacing. He tried to push them aside but they wouldn't go away. Idiot! How could he have wasted a whole afternoon hanging out at Garth's? The need to know if Laura was alright had become a fire alarm jangling in his head.

Volleyball practice for the Southmead Storm girls' rep team would be at the school gym. Mom wouldn't take him, no point asking. He'd have to ride his bike. Really, dipshit,? Three kilometres on snow-covered roads? Walk instead? It was already past seven — he had to get there. It was bike or nothing.

Lyle shrugged on the parka and mitts he wore for mornings waiting on the school bus in the frigid darkness. He headed for the back door. "Mom, gotta go out, forget supper," he yelled, slammed the door without waiting for an answer, ran to the garage and grabbed his bike.

Dad had got it for him, a mountain bike with knobbly tires, not long before he went away. It could handle the winter roads in a pinch, but was hardly ideal transport at this hour, lacking lights.

A bitter night, no wind for once. No moon either. Instead, an endless canopy of stars, enough to light the way as Lyle's eyes adjusted. The spectacle caught his attention and brought to mind a TV program about galaxies and the Big Bang and stuff. Here it all was, right there above him, and for a moment the reality of it was almost scary. Here he was, biking across the flatlands by the light of a billion suns. Sorta awesome, he'd have to tell Garth about it, the little nerd got off on that kind of thing. Then images of Laura being used by Brad and Mitch returned and eclipsed the majesty of the Universe.

A couple of vehicles passed going his way but nobody stopped to offer a ride. Which they could have, a pickup and an SUV after all. Lyle didn't care, he could do this, was *going* to do this. A hard knot of purpose had formed. Wheeling through the freezing darkness, he'd embraced a mission. The women he cared about needed help and he would find a way to bring it. And right then, his distress about being the not-totally-up-to-the-task younger brother fell away, no longer shadowing him like an unwelcome revenant. It felt strange, yet free, and he pedalled on.

The deep insistent drumming of a locomotive sounded across the fields. Lyle approached the railway crossing. His leg muscles had begun to burn but time was short and the approaching train would be one of those mile-long freights that took forever to pass. He stood up on the pedals and made all deliberate speed toward the tracks. The air started vibrating.

No problem, he'd make it with a good hundred meters to spare. He sped up to the crossing, the locomotive's siren deep and urgent in his ears. The barriers had come down and the red lights flashed a warning. No problem again, a quick zig around the barriers and he'd be by.

The train's headlight was a staring white eye getting larger by the second. The bike's front wheel hit a skim of ice and Lyle slammed down hard, sprawling between the tracks. The siren sounded staccato, urgent blasts. Lyle's left leg got hooked through the bike's frame and it was taking way too long to drag free. The train had become a child's nightmare monster bent on ending his life but in the final panicked moments he managed to free his leg and scrabble, crabwise crawling, across the last rail. He barely had time to twist around and watch the locomotive thunder past, shaking the ground.

Every part of him felt like Jell-O. His leg hurt bad. Freight cars rumbled by, *that close*, stirring up gusts of cold air. The bike was gone.

Headlights, a car door opening, a voice calling, "Jesus, kid, are you alright?" Footsteps approached and Lyle rolled over. A broad-shouldered male figure approached. The guy squatted down beside him. "Can I check you over? I've had some training. Stay still. Where are you hurting?"

Despite the shock and a feeling like somebody sticking a screwdriver into his leg, Lyle was relieved that the guy was focusing on his injuries, not on what he'd stupidly done. But he'd messed up again, hadn't he? Where was the warrior-on-a-mission from a few short minutes ago?

Not utterly gone missing. "I'm good thanks," he managed to gasp between shaky breaths, heart galloping in his chest, "just banged up a bit. Need to be somewhere, over at the school, gotta get there. Help me up."

Holding onto the man's arm, Lyle got on one knee, then pulled himself to his feet. His leg throbbed and stung. He screwed up his face at the pain.

The man shook his head. "Where d'you live? The only place you need to go is home. What were you doing out here anyway, riding a bike in the middle of winter and nearly getting yourself killed?"

"I have to get to the school. There's this girl I have to talk to."

"Wow, kid, she must be pretty special, but talk to her tomorrow. Come on, get in the car. You're going home."

"No, Sir. I truly appreciate it but I gotta keep going. It's not far, I can make it."

"Are you crazy? That's a kilometre at least through town. And the leg of yours is hurtin' I can tell."

After a couple more tries, Lyle not giving way, the man blew out air and agreed to take Lyle where he wanted to go. Outside school, Lyle thanked his Good Samaritan and shook hands. "You're welcome," the man told him. "Go on then, I hope she's worth it."

Lyle made it round to the gym, pretty much hopping on one leg. Here was Darlene's Volleyball team in the hallway. He was momentarily distracted from the stabbing in his shin by an abundance of ponytails, long legs and cute bums. Darlene was there, flushed and sweaty with her mop of dark hair and full figure.

He approached her, "Darlene, can I talk to you? It's about Laura." She got the privacy message and they moved off down the hall, the other girls giving sideways stares. "Darlene, maybe you think this is, I dunno, inappropriate, but can I get Laura's number off you? Like, I'm really scared about her and you must be too, and I know you think I'm like, a total dick, but…"

Darlene's expression went unreadable, then it changed to horror. "Lyle, what's happened to you? Have you been in a fight?"

"Nah, came off my bike and wrecked it."

"Omigod there's blood all down your pant leg!"

"Only a scratch. Look, can I get Laura's number Darlene, please?"

Darlene shook her head. "We promised each other never to give out our numbers, especially to boys. Can't do it."

What teenage dreamworld was the girl living in?

"Darlene, get real, will you? Laura's disappeared, who knows where or why, but if she still has her phone maybe we could find out if she's okay. Her parents said she left a note and they're hoping maybe she's just taken off somewhere."

"No, Lyle, you get real! Don't you think I've tried to call her? Don't you think her parents have? She's not answering, okay? So no, I told you already, I'm not giving you her number."

The hallway started revolving and Lyle found himself sitting on the floor. Darlene and her mother stood whispering to each other and glancing sideways at him, concern written on their faces. Several members of the volleyball team were clustered behind them in their skimpy black outfits, still staring. Darlene's Mom turned out to be the take-charge sort and Lyle was past protesting. Along with her daughter she helped him to an old blue Minivan and off they went to Southmead Health Centre, a barebones two-room facility with one duty nurse-practitioner, Jean, and Wally, retired cop, dozing at the security station.

Jean didn't like the look of Lyle's leg. It was swelling up and she told him he might have a fracture.

"Probably the fibula, if it was the tibia, you wouldn't have been able to walk, it must hurt a lot as it is."

Oh it hurt, alright. Jean gave him painkillers and got him as comfortable possible on a gurney.

"The on-duty doc will be here shortly. Who can we call? Your parents?"

Darlene and her Mom were hovering. "We can take him home after he's seen the doc," Ms Falconer told the nurse.

"It's okay," Lyle said, "my Mom can come, I'll call her. And thanks, Ms Falconer, for looking after me and getting me here." Her daughter not so much. They took their leave, heading down the hallway in an intense whispered exchange. Jean insisted on making the call home and got no answer. Lyle wanted to kick himself. Mom was most likely passed out on her wine and a joint again, like yesterday. She thought he didn't know about the Pot. Like, he couldn't smell it, hello?

Jean was off to attend another client, an older woman with chest pains by the sound of it.

"We'll deal with transport later." she told him, "Let's see what the doc has to say about your leg. That's the number one priority. He's on his way." Lyle closed his eyes. What a pathetic waste of time, loser. Wrecked his bike as well, all for nothing.

A voice jerked him awake. "Mr Prince, we meet for the second time today. What have you been up to now?" Lyle took a couple of seconds to grasp where he was. Looking down at him was Laura's father, Dr MacDonald. Lyle explained how he'd come off his bike, omitting the close encounter with the locomotive and death. His listener did not appear totally convinced, but let it pass and examined the leg.

"Lyle, try pointing your toe for me."

Gingerly, Lyle tried. A jolt of electric pain lanced up his shin. It took his breath away and he broke out in a sweat.

"Yup, Jean was right, you have what we call a greenstick fracture, not a complete break. You're going to get a cast, right away. She's busy, I'll do it, stay put." Lyle had no problem complying.

Half an hour later, fibreglass cast in place, crutch provided, transport home was back on the agenda. Mom still did not answer, which was just as well because she'd be in no condition to drive anyway. Dr MacDonald offered a ride. Could this be another opportunity to complete the mission? Play it careful.

They drove through town in awkward silence. Laura's disappearance hovered between them. Lyle shut his eyes when the railroad crossing came up. Then they were past. MacDonald cleared his throat.

"Lyle, what were you doing riding your bike into town in the middle of winter. Seems like a rather unwise thing to do?"

"Sir, I wanted to get Laura's number off Darlene, and I found her but she wouldn't give it to me. Is Laura alright? Have you heard from her?"

Dr MacDonald's answer came out flat. Lyle noticed his hands clasping and unclasping on the steering wheel. "We haven't spoken to her, but we've had a couple of text messages saying she is okay and don't worry. Says she's safe where she is. What does *that* mean? It's bizarre! If she was home with us she *wouldn't* be safe? How can we not be worried out of our minds? This is so unlike her and terribly upsetting, especially to her mother. And the thing is, how do we know the messages are really from her? We don't get to hear her voice. So we asked what was the name of her teddy bear? And the right answer came back, but how do we know it wasn't somebody making her tell? I guess at least it means she's alive. Oh, God."

Lyle could imagine what this must be like. He remembered the night Kenny'd been taken away in the ambulance fighting for his life. And losing.

Move on. "So what are the cops doing? Anything?"

"I suppose. Harrington tells me every one of his officers is on the lookout, but I know these guys. They've convinced themselves it's simply a teenage crisis. They think the text messages are genuine. We don't know what to do, Lyle, we honestly don't. Her mother is beside herself. Me too." Dr McDonald rubbed a hand across his face.

It was a new experience, Dr MacDonald talking to him man to man this way. Lyle badly wanted to respond, and not like some dopey kid. The whole thing was simply not right. Nobody should have to go through this. Not Laura's parents, not the annoying Darlene, not him. Lyle had set out on a mission tonight, and the night wasn't over. He was about to open his mouth when Dr MacDonald saved him the trouble.

"So you wanted Laura's number? Why not call us?"

"Sir, I didn't think you'd give it out, to be honest. I owe your daughter for what she did calling the cops that night at the Mini Mart. Another girl might have thought, oh not my problem. But not Laura, and now she's in some kind of trouble and maybe it's because of that. And now I think if I'd, you know, left it and not gotten involved with those jerks, well, I want to help Laura any way I can, you know?"

"And this couldn't wait 'till tomorrow?"

"No, Sir, it couldn't."

"Well, Mr Prince, it may not do any good but I tell you what, right now your offer of help is appreciated and accepted. Get out your phone and I'll give you my baby's number."

***

Judy awoke at the sound of a car door. After Lyle had taken off, her only option that evening had been to sit there, slumped in front of the TV with a bottle of wine, and wonder where her son had gone, and why. She checked the clock and it told her she'd been out of it for two hours. Her mouth felt like sandpaper and compost.

A key turned in the front door. Lyle limped in followed by Dr MacDonald. The doctor's presence brought Judy wide awake. She took in Lyle's condition, the crutch, the torn bloody pant leg, and let out a wail of dismay.

"Oh my dear child, what's happened to you? Who did this?"

No longer was he the pain-in-the-ass useless kid, he was the son she'd brought into this world and whoever'd done this was going to suffer the flaming intensity of his mother's wrath.

Dr MacDonald stepped forward. He explained the source of Lyle's injuries, and the purpose of his errand into town. Judy rubbed her forehead. She didn't get it. The whole thing seemed so unlike Lyle. Never mind that. She hustled off into the kitchen and made him a hot chocolate. Dr MacDonald warned her not to give him any more painkillers tonight, but he opened up his bag and pulled out a small brown bottle.

"These will help with the pain," he told Judy. "Start them tomorrow. They'll last a couple of days, then we'll see. Now I really should get back. And while riding his bike through the snow-covered roads wasn't the smartest thing, your son is a determined little cuss, I have to say."

The fear and concern were back on his face. "We've heard from Laura. At least we think it's her. But it's only text messages. No matter how we beg, she won't call. If we could only hear her voice…"

He pursed his lips. "I gotta go."

One part of Judy wanted to interrogate her son. She had a feeling he'd been up to something more than what she'd been told. Could he have gotten all messed up like that from falling off his bike? Where was it anyway? That was a good bike. Surely Lee could fix it? And what good would it do him to have Laura's number?

The interrogation, if there was to be one, would have to wait. For the first time in a while Judy wanted to be kind to her son, to mother him and make it better.

"Come on," she said, "let's get you into bed, and I'll have those pants off you. They're going in the garbage."

"Mom, something else happened today. I tried to tell you before. I spoke to Dad."

"Did you now? And I'm guessing your new best pal Monty set that up?"

"Yeah, Mom, he did. And Dad told me about Hank Niles, and Billy, and why Billy doesn't like us, and how Billy put him inside. Did you know about that?"

Mom crouched down beside where Lyle lay on the sofa.

"You need to go to bed Lyle. Yes I knew. We'll talk tomorrow."

They made it to Lyle's room. Mom got him undressed and into bed. He was too exhausted to get all embarrassed.

"Call me if you need anything. Anything at all, okay?"

Judy leaned in and gave her son a hug. She breathed the familiar boy-smell of hair needing a wash and the hard-to-place slightly sour young-man odour she remembered from way back with boys in cars. Well there you go, what goes around comes around. She put her hand on her son's arm. He gave a sniff and a little grunt and fell asleep.

He looked so peaceful and innocent. She hoped she'd be able hold on to that image

11. A CONVERSATION

Billy Niles did not want to be here.

The Sunrise canning plant stood in open country twenty kilometres out of Southmead. A brick-chimneyed relic of post-World-War-II expansion, it was closing in on the end of its life, which was why it had been chosen. A thin ribbon of steam rose from an outbuilding, the only sign the place wasn't derelict.

Billy tried to reassure himself with the thought that few people would be around. With luck, under cover of darkness, anybody spotting him would take him for a sidekick, bagman for Warren McKaskell, head honcho at Sunrise Foods. He chewed on a fingernail. The guy was supposed to have been here ten minutes ago.

The rental car Billy'd arrived in was probably a useless precaution but why give the security cameras, if there were any, an easy shot? He wore dark clothes and had a mesh cap ready on the passenger seat. McKaskell had been cagey about his reasons for wanting a meeting tonight, here of all places, but he'd given Billy no option. Billy didn't like being backed into a corner and he had come prepared.

Was his scheme with McKaskell going to work? The processing industry cartel's loathing of the Co-op was no secret. Seeing it closed down or under trusteeship of the hard-right provincial government would be a prize worth a substantial reward. Such had been the message, communicated through intermediaries, more often than not on the golf course — the perfect venue for deniable conversations. The message had come at a bad time. Or maybe a good time depending on how you looked at it, because Billy had been desperate.

He'd come to detest his job, sick of the Chicken Charlies who had to be placated and pandered-to. He despised the rubes who paid their *donations* and never had the balls to protest. But sooner or later, he was sure, the permit-selling shakedown was going to blow up, so he was in a fix. He'd come to depend on it to keep Clara in the style she enjoyed.

A couple of months back, word had reached Billy about a libertarian faction in the Co-op. They'd started muttering and speculating about an *occupation* like the one in Oregon. Come like shadows in the night, barricade the place and take a stand to protest the plight of the family farm. Crazy? Absolutely, but here was a way out, and Billy'd opened negotiations with McKaskell.

A sleek Lexus pulled alongside and McKaskell appeared. Billy got out of the rental, greeted him and they shook. McKaskell was clad in high-end winter outdoorwear, like you'd see at Blue Mountain or Whistler.

"So here we are, William. I appreciate you making the time for this meeting," McKaskell was a big guy, his voice deep and resonant with the casual drawl of the super-rich: domed forehead, heavy features and wavy black hair left a little too long. Not exactly what you'd expect from the boss of an agribusiness conglomerate, but blood, not talent, had put McKaskell in charge. Sunrise was a family concern.

Billy was in no mood for social niceties "No problem, Warren, though I have to tell you, it's beyond me why you've got us trekking out here in the freezing goddamn cold on a weekend." He pulled the ball-cap lower on his face.

"Nonsense, William, I can't think of a better place for a last-minute conference. Besides, something's come up and we need to talk."

Billy balled his fists. This was how Warren did deals. The old bait-and-switch. Catch the other guy off balance. You'd expect it from a huckster in a leather jacket selling dodgy goods out the back of a truck, but the head honcho at Sunrise Foods?

And did the fool ever listen, Billy wondered. All McKaskell wanted was to bring down the Co-op, but the risks they were both taking obviously weren't real to him. He decided not to respond directly. The panicky feeling from this morning was back. It was becoming only too clear that his partner in this caper, and future benefactor if it all panned out, was treating it way too much like another piece of corporate maneuvering.

He took a deep breath. "Are we going inside then, or what?"

*

A pulsing stabbing pain in Lyle's shin woke him — useless painkillers! Confused images of the previous day came and went, mixed with fears and speculation. He remembered the call with Dad. Hank had to have been on his way home from the barn, Dad had said — the one with two silos at the turnoff, where criminal plans were hatched. What could that mean? In a half awake and confused state though he was, one thought wouldn't go away. He had to check out that barn. And was it a dream, or was it what Garth had said, because, as it seemed to Lyle, Laura's disappearance was somehow connected.

Laura. He had her phone number now. So why haven't you texted her, dummy? He carefully rolled over. Shit, where was his phone? Had he wrecked it falling off his bike? At that moment he could imagine nothing worse. No, stupid, you had it when you got the number from her dad. He gritted his teeth and ever so gently swung his feet to the floor. Diesel showed up on his nightly patrol and, with the contrariness of cats, rubbed against the sore leg. Lyle crawled out to the coat closet, hauled himself up, and dug in the pocket of his parka. His fingers closed on the phone. He pulled it out. The face was intact. Back in his room, come on, he told it, turn on! It did, and Lyle went giddy with relief. Then it chimed. He had messages.

Now Lyle put together how Laura was keeping her whereabouts secret. He knew from the Sally Barnes episode that a cellphone could be tracked, but turned off or flat battery, and no way they could track you. She was keeping the phone off except for a quick texting session, or whoever had her was. Who'd been texting him?

Garth, sent at 11pm:

U awake?

Then a string of messages:

No ur not

Sirens downtown WTF

U ok?

Lyle sent his first ever text: *got hurt ned 2 sleep talk tmrw.*

The leg started throbbing again. Lyle fell back into bed in hopes of getting back to sleep. Oh shit. He'd forgotten his whole purpose, to contact Laura.

The phone's screen flashed "Low Battery. Charge your phone now." Lyle wanted to throw it across the room but that wouldn't be the smart thing to do. Out of bed again, leg giving him the cold sweats, find the charger in his backpack, plug it in.

Yr dad gave me yr number. Hope ur ok. think i know why you hiding. Want to help.

Lyle waited crouched against the wall by the power outlet. Come on Laura, answer! Minutes went by and no chime. Leave it on in case. Then his thoughts turned to that guy Niles. He opened up his laptop and Googled Billy Niles.

The first thing to come up was a homepage boasting about the Co-op's wonderful protection for the family farm, including a picture of the fearless leader grinning like a chimpanzee. It made Lyle want to gag. Scroll down. Here was something, a press article, *The Beacon: Co-op Boss Cleared of Extortion*. Complaints had been made, the piece said, but at a preliminary hearing a certain Mitchell Bigelow had denied every last suggestion put to him and that had been the end of it.

Dad had been right. Niles was in deep. Now Lyle had a third mission. He stored up the anger for when he'd need it.

Back to bed. He was done.

*

McKaskell and Billy sauntered through the dark canning plant. Billy'd been here before but never at night. The interior, dimly lit by safety-lights, looked like some kind of ancient industrial hellhole: looming shapes of vats, boilers, conveyors, a carousel filled with jars. They entered a long room with metal-topped tables. The air reeked of vinegar.

They arrived at the loading bays. McKaskell parked himself on a bench and motioned Billy to join him. He pulled out a hip flask, unscrewed the cup, poured a shot of amber liquid and passed the cup to Billy. McKaskell took a pull from the flask. Billy raised the cup and downed the shot.

McKaskell smacked his lips. "Ah, yes! Alberta Premium one hundred percent Canadian Rye. Another?"

Billy held out the cup and decided to sip it this time. He felt a little more amicable, but…

"Alright Warren, what's this about? It's a bit late for second thoughts, my friend."

McKaskell stared at the floor and sucked his teeth.

"We've received a decent offer for some of the equipment. They want the boilers and the two carousels. We need to put this whole thing on hold for a month or two. If they get messed up during your little demonstration it'll kill any deal, obviously."

Billy wanted to smack himself on the forehead and jump up and down. Instead he took a moment to finish his drink, calm himself and organize his answer. Appeals to the guy's intelligence would be a waste of breath. Telling him there was no way to stop the occupation at this point would be a last resort, but it might come to that.

"Warren, there's no need to worry. There's never been any intention to damage the place. It would only make the guys look bad — it won't happen."

McKaskell gave a low chuckle, expressing, better than any words, exactly what he thought of Billy's assurance.

"William, I've been checking on these people. Your pal with the chicken farm, for one. He's on Facebook, did you know?"

Oh shit. Billy had never suspected, never imagined.

"He's a whack job," McKaskell went on. "Some of the stuff on there is plain fucking mental. Reads like the dawn of the revolution. You better check out who you've gotten in bed with, my friend. No way am I letting that guy in here. Can't risk it."

Billy knew he was in bed with the wrong person alright. He struggled to grasp the depth of McKaskell's naiveté in thinking he could back out at the eleventh hour, and Charlie Webb's stupidity too. He took a couple of deep breaths. This would not be a good moment to lose it.

"See, Warren," he said, "maybe I should remind you of our agreement. I've done what I promised. The radicals in the Co-op are going to occupy the plant to protest the plight of the small farmer. No damage, nobody gets hurt, but the Co-op gets discredited and disbanded. In return I receive a consulting contract to compensate me for the risks I've taken and the stress I've endured to make this happen. And let's not forget the payout to my helpers. That would be Mitch, Brad, Bert, and yes even Charlie, remember? They would be seriously upset if you stiffed them, I can tell you."

McKaskell didn't answer. Billy decided to keep after him.

"And what was it you told me? For the Co-op to go away is worth fifteen mil a year to your processors' cartel? Pretty good return on investment, I should say."

McKaskell turned, his face filled with suspicion. "William, are you wearing a wire?"

Billy returned the look. "No. Should I be? Because you're really pissing me off with these last-minute out-of-the blue demands you know damn well I can't meet. I don't control these people. Never claimed I did. The occupation is going to happen. You hear me?"

"Great, now you tell me. Last time we met, it was, *No problem Warren, leave everything to me, these guys eat out of my hand.*"

"I never said any such thing. When did I say that? You're making stuff up!"

"Doesn't matter anyway. You think it can't be stopped? Did you honestly think I wouldn't have a contingency plan? That's how you survive in business, my friend. Because I can shut the whole thing down with one phone call. Our security firm will have their guys here ready and waiting. End of story."

Billy shook his head in disbelief. He should have seen this coming. McKaskell was turning out to be dumber than a pile of rocks. He tried, with only partial success, to keep his voice even, give it one last shot.

"And when the whole business turns into a cluster fuck, shots fired, people hurt, or worse, which it will, mark my words, what do you think your toy soldiers are gonna tell the cops? Who ordered them here and for what purpose, of course. You think they're gonna keep your name out of it? Dream on, Warren. I sure hope you have a good lawyer. You better think about this very carefully. We can both go down together or we can stay clear and let the occupation take its course. When it's done I'll wring my hands at the actions of a few hotheads, the Co-op will be history, and you'll have your excuse to close the plant and sell the equipment. These guys aren't out to wreck the place, it'll be fine!"

McKaskell sucked his teeth, again. The habit was getting on Billy's nerves.

"Tomorrow night, correct?"

Billy nodded.

"And no damage, you say?"

"Right. That would only make them look like a bunch of vandals, not poor hardworking farmers seeking justice, like I told you before."

The Chief Executive Officer of Sunrise foods said nothing for several minutes. The only sound was a steady dripping from the gallery next door. McKaskell gave a sniff. "Alright, but I'm uncomfortable with this. We're not where I'd expected we'd be at this eleventh hour."

Billy stood. Be gracious. "Warren, I understand your concerns, but this is not a win-lose. It's a win-win. You've made the right decision. I appreciate the opportunity to reassure you."

"William, I'm not reassured, okay? And if there's damage done, then I won't feel obliged to award you the consulting contract. Your little victory here today could end up costing you. Remember that." McKaskell turned on his heel and headed for the exit, swaggering a little, probably because he figured he'd gotten the last word.

Billy followed, going over the whole exchange in his mind. The sonofabitch still reckoned he held the high cards, didn't he? He pulled out his phone and ended the recording. You had to protect yourself when dealing with a piece of work like McKaskell.

Warren McKaskell made his way outside, muttering under his breath. The plan he'd cooked up wasn't going to work. In the car, after a brief debate with himself, he called a number he preferred to use as little as possible.

"You were right. It's too late to put the whole thing off. Your buddy was a total pain in the ass."

"He's not my buddy, I told you that before," Mitch Bigelow replied.

"Whatever. Anyway, looks like we go to plan B tomorrow. You still up for it?"

"No problem. Plan B it is."

"Can you get word out to the troops to stand down?"

"Christ no, Warren! Screw them. Some dopey shit'll open their mouth to Niles. That's the last thing we want."

12. TEXTS AND PICKLE JARS

Laura flipped on the bedside light. Trickles of condensation ran down the yellowed walls. The air stank of mold. She checked her watch, six-thirty, her second morning holed up in the Falconers' RV and another hour before Darlene would sneak her a mug of tea and something to eat.

She was in a pretty good funk, what with frantic texts from her parents, fear she'd be found by the crazies planning the occupation, and the chill in the RV with its puny electric heater. Running away had seemed the only option after Darlene's confession at the Dairy Queen. So, when Darlene and her mom had offered refuge in the RV at their small holding she'd gone for it. But now she understood. Poor Mom and Dad, worried sick. What a thoughtless, selfish daughter she was.

Adding to her distress, a question kept gnawing at her. Why had Darlene and her mom got her here, really? Was it only about keeping her safe? Or was hiding her meant to protect Darlene's dad as well?

He would never know she was here, they'd told her, because the RV was stored in a shed, down a track away from the house. Laura had promised to keep her phone turned off apart from texts to assure her parents that she was alive and safe. Yet even as she made the promise, she'd known perfectly well that if she broke it, Darlene and her mom would be none the wiser. What option did they have, anyway? If they'd tried to take her phone, it would have confirmed she was a prisoner. Well, was she?

Should she call Mom and Dad right now? Why not call the police and blow the whole thing wide open? Stuck here in the RV, she'd gone over this about a million times. What it came down to was that she didn't want to get Darlene in trouble. The processing plant she could care less about. Maybe the crazies even had a case.

Another uncomfortable thought struck her. Had Darlene been telling the truth that night at the Dairy Queen? Not about the occupation — that part Laura could believe, but about the crazies she needed to hide from?

"Oh, Dar," she whispered, "what have you got me into?"

*

Lyle's leg didn't hurt so bad this morning. Maybe the painkillers had worked after all, but he needed to go to the can. He rolled over, carefully, reached for the crutch, hauled himself out of bed, the leg less happy now, and limped to the washroom. He managed to keep his aim inside the rim, not so easy while balanced on a crutch, then checked his phone. It was charged, so he unplugged it from the wall and took it back to bed. Nothing from Laura.

Two hours later, Lyle was starting to grasp the depth of his predicament. Getting showered, dried and dressed had needed help from Mom, and visions of a speedy recovery to regular mobility had evaporated. Mom served up oatmeal followed by scrambled eggs and smoked sausage, way better than the usual. The expected interrogation didn't materialize. She left with a promise to be back by noon. And the whole while, Laura was on his mind. What should he be doing that he'd either not thought of, or couldn't do anyway with his bum leg?

Then, hold on, Lyle, he thought, take a break, this is so not your problem. You've got yourself all messed up over a girl who thinks you're a total dick. How pathetic is that? Wake up and get a life. If the stupid girl's taken off, what are you supposed to do about it? The sentiment lasted all of ten seconds.

He flopped down on the couch and checked his phone. Still no text from Laura. The phone trilled. Was it her? No, Garth.

"What's happening?" Garth asked. "What's this about getting hurt? You got my texts from last night, right?"

"Yes Garth, to both questions. I came off my bike and wrecked my leg, okay? So I'm half way crippled and stuck here at home talking to you. Are you coming over and help me or you gonna hang there at school and try to talk to girls?"

"It's Sunday you moron. I'll ask Father for a ride. Get back to you."

Five minutes later, text incoming:

There in 20

Next priority, Laura or Marigold? Lyle couldn't help it, he had to try Laura again with another text. Kind of like fishing. You might not catch anything but you sure wouldn't if you didn't get a hook in the water. What about bait then? A fish wouldn't take an empty hook. He twisted around, stuck his feet on the couch and began stabbing at the tiny keypad.

Sorry I pd you off at school. Am idiot. We never had that pizza. Can I make it right?

Lyle, he said to himself, that is so lame. He was about to ditch the text, but reconsidered, sighed, and hit *send* instead.

Next, check in with Marigold, see what she knew about the sirens Garth had reported in Southmead. She picked up on the second ring. "Lyle, good morning to you. What has you calling me this not-so-lovely morning in this shitty little town of yours?"

"Hey, don't be mad at *me*. Something happen?"

"Something sure did. My frickin' car got torched right in the motel parking lot. Lyle, cars don't go up in flames on their own, you know?"

Oh yes, he knew. The bad stuff was coming fast now, like that freight train. Alarm bells started ringing in his head louder than ever. Please let Laura be hiding and not a prisoner, but right then he knew, just knew, that Garth was right. It was all connected. People who would torch a car might do anything. The best place for Laura, the dummy, was home with her parents. The need to make that happen was all he could think about now, even if she did think he was a dick.

"Lyle? You still there?"

"Uh, yeh, sorry, and that's awful about your car. Are you okay?"

"Totally fine. People want to scare me off, bring it on. They picked the wrong woman to mess with. They'll see. Assholes, I was fond of that Nissan. Now, back to my question. What do you have for me this morning?"

"I got the contact number for the missing girl, Laura. So I've texted her in hopes she can answer. Not much, I guess, but I don't know what else to do. The other thing is, I learned stuff about that guy Niles who was at court last week. Things that might interest you. Wanna hear?"

"You bet, I'm very much interested in that gentleman but, um, maybe not over the phone. I have some news for you too. Can we meet?"

"I messed up my leg so I'm stuck at home." Lyle remembered his excuse to Ms Wynne for skipping Phys Ed. The ironies of life.

"Okaay..." Marigold sounded like she was making plans. "I've got a rental car coming. Then I have a visit to make. After that I could stop by if you want and you can give me the skinny. You up for that?"

"Sure, 79 Mary Street, north out of town. Can you find it?"

"No problem, the rental comes with GPS. Hang loose, I'll be there in a while."

*

The ringing clatter of pickle jars jostling down the canning plant's conveyor turned Bert Falconer's headache into a jangling migraine. Time-and-a-half for working Sunday? Triple time wouldn't be enough right now. He finished packing another dozen jars, taped the carton closed and slapped it on the skid with the previous thirty-something.

Where the hell could Darlene's buddy Laura have got to? Had she blabbed to the cops? Would he and his mates arrive at the plant tonight and walk into an ambush? It would be his fault. That could not be allowed to happen.

Bert had interrogated his daughter that morning as she lounged in bed, grumpy at being disturbed early on a Sunday.

*

"Darlene, don't bullshit me, alright? You and Laura can never get your faces out of your damn phones. So where is she?"

Darlene folded her arms and her face went tight. "Dad, I told you already. Didn't you hear me? Her phone doesn't answer. And what's the big deal for you anyway, Dad? You don't even like her."

Bert had made the mistake of yelling. "Because you went and told her about our demonstration, you halfwit little bitch! How do I know she isn't gonna tell?"

The shouting had brought his wife Louise pushing through the door and grabbing his arm. It went right away to shoving and screaming, Louise ended up with a black eye, again, and Bert none the wiser. Did Laura know that he knew that she knew — jeez it sounded like a cheesy sitcom — had Darlene told her that too? It stood to reason. Laura MacDonald was hiding somewhere, fearful that someone would try to shut her up. Where could she be? She couldn't have called the cops or they'd have been on him like bugs on roadkill. Was there still time to find her and get her to keep quiet, or make damn sure she would?

*

The jars started backing up on the belt and Bert's co-worker Eileen called out, "Hey, Bert, get the lead out willya!"

Goddamn Eileen. Goddamn dill pickles.

As he shoved jars into the next carton, Bert remembered something he'd seen earlier that morning, something out of place but at the time he couldn't put his finger on it. Footprints maybe? Pulling out from home, his glance had crossed the track that led down to the shed where the RV and mower were stored for the winter. In his mind's eye now he saw it, fresh footprints in the snow, leading from the house across to the shed, where footprints had no reason to be.

13. MARIGOLD'S NEWS

Garth arrived right after Marigold. She came equipped with coffee and Garth said he wasn't thirsty so Lyle was relieved of hospitality obligations to either one. They took seats in the living room and contemplated each other in a questioning silence. Garth, unusual for him, broke it.

He pointed to the leg. "What incredibly dumb act of poor judgement caused *that*?" Lyle was ready for the question and gave much the same version as he'd given Mom, with emphasis on the triumph of getting Laura's phone number but omitting the freight train. One day, not today though, he might tell Garth the whole story.

"So did you call her yet?" Garth said.

"I texted her. I'm guessing she has her phone turned off most of the time, so no answer. Not yet anyway."

"Do not hold your breath waiting on that young woman, you could suffocate."

Yeah, get over it Garth. Couldn't he see that Laura was no threat to their friendship? Forget about it. Let her be alright.

Marigold spoke up. "Lyle, can we get to Laura in a minute? I've learned a couple of things, but I thought it was going to be just the two of us. Can I share?" She avoided eye-contact with Garth, who returned the favour and examined the wall.

"Absolutely, Garth is my best friend and knows everything I do, so no problem. Please, what have you found out? Anything about Mom?"

"Before we get to that, both of you, I have a source to protect. You speak to anyone, anyone at all, about what I'm gonna tell you now, and my source will be in big trouble. So will you. You got that?"

Garth nodded, mute.

"Tell me yes, I wanna hear you say it."

"Yes."

"Alright, sorry Lyle, not much news about your mom yet. The cops are still checking out the wreck of Hank Niles' car. He had summer tires, and no anti-lock brakes on an old car like that of course, but they're still looking. Back on the hill, they couldn't find any trace of the brakes being applied. My source says they really want to pin that on your mom. The Coroner is waiting on the postmortem from Kincardine, but for now that's it."

He nodded. "Sure, Marigold, I get it. Thanks for the update anyway. Keep me posted, okay?"

"Will do. Your turn."

Disappointment had left Lyle in a moment of blankness. What else had he promised Marigold? His leg pulsed from sitting too long in one position and he shifted around on the sofa. Diesel arrived, licking his chops from a late breakfast, ignored Marigold and hopped up on the arm of Garth's chair to be petted. Garth obliged.

Marigold waited, regarding Lyle with those deep brown eyes under raised brows. Then he remembered — the call with Dad. He took a second to collect his thoughts. "I have a source I can't name, like you do. This is about Billy Niles."

"Go on."

Lyle explained what Dad had told him about the permit-selling shakedown.

Marigold nodded like this was no surprise. "You have a good source there, Lyle. This confirms what I suspected. But we can't publish without proof or the paper would get sued and I'd be jobless. But this is still great collateral. I'm going to keep digging. Trash my car? Bad idea, guys. Very bad idea."

Marigold was some kind of impressive woman, different than any Lyle had come across. She had a feisty, youthful energy about her. She opened up new possibilities about what a woman could be. Lyle's mind turned to Laura. To him she was already perfect. What sort of woman she might become was beyond his imagination.

"Earth to Lyle. Is that it?" Marigold said.

Lyle's Daydreams of Laura evaporated. "My source told me something else. There's a barn way out of town where dirtbags used to hang out, maybe still do. Guess what, the hill where Hank had his crash is right on the shortest route between town and that barn. So what do you think about that?"

Marigold did her big-eyes look again. "Omigod, Lyle, this could make a difference, get the cops' minds off your mom."

Garth took a break from petting Diesel. "See, like I told you, it's all connected. And here we have another piece of the puzzle. This barn is obviously bad-guy HQ. Come on, we have to go check it out." He made to rise from his chair, as animated as Lyle had ever seen him. Marigold held up a hand. "Hold on there, soldier! This is another thing we need to tell the police. I can't be withholding critical information. I'd be protecting criminals for the sake of a story. I won't do that, sorry."

Well, get her, Ms I'm so pure and righteous.

"Excuse me?" Lyle said, "What was that about protecting sources? Is that only good for yours? What about mine? And what would you tell the cops anyway? *Oh, there's this barn where crooks used to hang out?* Like, you think they don't already know that? And even if they don't, are they gonna get all armoured up and go busting in there? You think?"

The pair of them were looking at him, not exactly open-mouthed but definitely paying attention.

"So yeah, I'm with Garth, I want to check that place out. If Hank was there right before he died, you're right, that could be huge for Mom. But what do we do? Show up and hope nobody's around?"

Garth stood and began pacing, shaking his head. Marigold stayed quiet, glancing between the two of them. After a bit she drained her coffee and set down the cup. "Forget that for one minute. I've got one last bit of news. I'm sorry Lyle, I meant to tell you this upfront. On my way here I knocked on some doors on Laura's street. There's a lady a few houses down from where Laura lives, opposite side of the street. She was just back from an overnight trip, so she hadn't heard about Laura going missing.

"She said that on Friday evening there was a Minivan parked across from her place, dark coloured, could have been blue. She didn't think anything about it, and later she heard it drive off. Not sure that means anything, but I thought I'd pass it along."

Lyle's brain lit up. "You're not sure it means anything? Are you kidding! Darlene, that's Laura's best friend, her mom drives a blue van. That's it!" He whipped out his phone and started texting.

Yr at Darlene's. Coming to get you.

14. BERT'S EXCUSE

No shower for two days, the only facilities a washbasin ringed with grime, and a revolting chemical toilet. Laura felt like she'd been here for weeks. The door of the shed rumbled open and Darlene showed up with what would have to pass for breakfast: a cup of tepid tea and a barely warm fried-egg sandwich. She sipped the tea anyway got up the nerve to ask the why-am-I-here-really question.

Darlene went quiet. "Don't know what you mean. Mom and me are risking our necks to keep you safe, and now you start asking why? You know why, so thanks Laura, and I'm sorry if your hair's all greasy because, no, you can't come in for a shower. Dad's at work but he could show up anytime."

Tense and closed-faced — this wasn't the usual Darlene.

"Oh, Dar," Laura said in her best trying-to-be-nice voice, "I didn't mean anything. Don't be mad at me, I guess I'm a bit stressed, you know?" Darlene wasn't having it. She shook her head and took off without another word. Laura brushed aside a cobweb, sat herself at the tiny table and took a bite at the sandwich.

What now? A wash in cold water? No thanks. She pulled a blanket around her shoulders. Come on Laura, she told herself, time to put your big girl pants on like Auntie Tina says. Do something, anything, because she couldn't face another day of this. Checking her phone would be a start. She turned it on. It chimed and a bunch of messages showed up. Two from her dad:

So very very concerned. Why would you do this. Please come home. Miss you darling girl.

Another Dad message. *Met yr friend Lyle Prince. Gave him yr number. He concerned too.*

Then, Lyle's texts.

He was coming to get her like a tarnished knight riding to the rescue! Oh don't be such a dope, she thought, but reading Lyle's message, Laura knew for sure that she was ready to leave, ready to be rescued if you could call it that. And the longer she stayed, didn't the chances of Mr Falconer finding her get worse? She answered Lyle's text.

***

Back at the Prince household, Lyle was practically jumping out of his seat, itching to get going, but Marigold had turned all weird and Mother-like.

"C'mon guys," she said, "we gotta let the police know about all this."

Involving the Southmead cops didn't sit right with Lyle. "Look," he said, "if Laura wanted the cops involved, she'd have called them from Darlene's. Let's, get over there right now. Then if she's not around, sure, we call the station. Can you live with that?"

Marigold threw up her hands. "Alright, you win, but we have to at least let Laura's parents know about the blue van."

"Yeah, I guess." Google found the home number. Marigold called, no reply.

As they got ready to leave for Darlene's, Lyle's phone chimed, a text from Laura: *ok come get me. In the shed down the laneway.*

He had to read it twice to make sure. A golden bubble of triumph exploded in his chest.

*

Bert Falconer made the excuse to his shift leader. "Family emergency, have to go, right now."

In the truck, he called Charlie. "I need a minder for somebody out at *The Keep*. Somebody with the sense to keep their hands off a young girl. Just till after tonight."

"Uh, Bert, why are you asking me? You think I'm like, an agency for protection services?"

A hum of frustration started in Bert's head. All he knew was he couldn't be the one to have blown the operation. His wife and daughter had hidden this Laura girl right under his nose, he'd bet on it.

Charlie was getting antsy. He asked the one question Bert didn't want to hear. "Is this about that girl that's gone missing? People go to jail for that. What's going on?"

"Charlie, you gotta help me out here. She needs protection whether she wants it or not. She knows about the operation and we gotta keep her quiet, you get it now?"

- 82 -

"Jesus, Bert! Now you tell me. How'd she find out? Who's been talking? Are we in the shit?"

Charlie's whiney voice had Bert feeling like his head was about to burst. "You know what, Charlie? I'll deal with it. Sorry I bothered ya, *pal*. Go see to yer fuckin' chickens." He wanted to slam down the phone, but all he could do was poke at the damn screen like some candy-ass hipster in a coffee shop.

*

The rumble from the door of the shed startled Laura. Had Darlene come back to make amends? Heavy footsteps. Someone trying the RV's door. A male voice, "Laura, are you in there?"

Omigod, think fast. "Mr Falconer, is that you?"

"Yes Laura, it's me. It's not safe for you here, I've come to take you where someone will look after you. I'm coming in."

"One minute, Mr Falconer, I'm just dressing. I want to go home now, please?" Oh no, wrong thing to ask. "Or, I mean, whatever. Give me a minute, alright?"

Laura fumbled for her phone. A voice in her head screamed escape. In the last year or so, Darlene's dad had started looking at her in *that* way. Protection? No thank *you*...forget texting, call somebody, quick. The number she hit was Lyle Prince's. The door handle turned.

*

Lyle's phone jangled—incoming voice call. Chauffeured by Marigold, Garth riding shotgun, they were headed across open country on icy back roads en-route to Darlene's. The call was from Laura but Lyle heard a man's voice, rough and threatening. "Give me that phone. Come on now, hand it over." He recognized the voice from last night's call to Darlene's.

The call ended.

Lyle steadied himself. He wasn't freaking out. That focussed, weird sense of urgent calm had returned.

"Marigold," he said, "somebody's found Laura. Somebody bad. Are we nearly there yet?"

Garth checked the GPS. "One minute, so what's the plan, Captain?"

Captain? Damn right, Captain he could be. He flashed on pedalling through the night toward the railway crossing. Don't mess up this time, you nob.

"Marigold, there's s'posed to be a track down to a shed, right by the

- 83 -

property. That's where she is, so drive in there and block it, okay?"

"You got it." Her reply carried fierce determination. Marigold wasn't coming across all mother-like now.

They came up on a turnoff to a snow-covered track a few yards down from the Falconers' Brookfield Road address. The house stood alone, a tired bungalow much like Lyle's, a good half mile from the next property. A shed stood at the end of the track, its doors open, a white pickup parked in front.

Marigold turned in too fast. The car fishtailed and slid sideways down a low bank. "Shit shit shit!" Marigold shoved the transmission into reverse and hit the gas. The only result was the whine of spinning tires.

Please not another fiasco. Lyle yanked the door open. "Garth," he said, "tell her how to rock it and get traction. I gotta go." He scrambled out and nearly fell as the crutch buried its foot in the snow.

"No, it's okay," Marigold called, "the rental guy gave me traction mats to put under the wheels in case I get stuck. They're in the trunk."

No time for that. There was movement by the shed. Sure enough, a golden-haired figure in jeans and the remembered puffy jacket was being helped into the truck by some guy, Darlene's father? No, not helped, shoved.

The door of the truck slammed and the engine roared to life. Lyle managed to scramble to the top of the snowbank. The truck started up the track, accelerating hard in a cloud of dark exhaust. Lyle stepped into its path, flung the crutch to the ground and raised his arms. A hand gripped his shoulder, Garth's voice, "I'm here." The truck kept coming but Lyle wasn't going to move. Think you can scare me off like a little kid, Bert Falconer, you miserable slime-ball? Try me. He focused on the truck, willed its suspension to collapse and its transmission to melt.

No such luck, the truck wasn't slowing, if anything it was speeding up. This was gonna be it, Lyle's last stand. His leg started to quiver and he was about five seconds away from messing his pants. Too bad. The way it looked now, he'd be dead before it happened.

The truck's horn was a continuous blare. Lyle put his hand over Garth's where it gripped his shoulder. "Sorry, guy," he muttered, but didn't think Garth heard. His last thought was, "Take care of yourself, Mom."

The onrushing truck slewed off the track and down the bank. Like last night in the school hallway, Lyle's legs went to Jell-O.

The next thing he knew, friendly voices were telling him it was okay.

Somebody was shouting. He opened his eyes and saw Darlene's dad running back toward the house. Warm breath caressed his cheek and he heard quiet words. "Thank you Lyle." It was Laura, here beside him, safe.

Lyle made it to a wobbly standing position with help from Garth and Laura. Shock and incredulity had them all speechless, not too surprising after Lyle and Garth nearly getting wiped out by a maniac in a pickup. Then everybody began talking at once.

Laura turned to Lyle. "Thank you, thank you, thank you! Omigod, Lyle, he told me he was taking me somewhere secure, but then, if you hadn't figured it out and come for me…"

"That guy was going to mow us down I believe," Garth said. "What happened?"

Lyle couldn't help himself. He reached out and took Laura's hand, "You grabbed the wheel, didn't you?"

Laura nodded, couldn't get words out.

Marigold jumped in. "Laura, time to call your folks, yeah?"

"Yes, but he took my phone."

Marigold offered hers and Laura made the call. "Oh, Dad, it's me. I'm okay and some amazing people have found me and I'm safe. I am so, so sorry. Yes it was Lyle who found me, how did you know?"

As she listened to her father's reply, Laura fixed a wide-eyed stare on Lyle. "So that's why you're limping! You messed up your leg to get my number! Yes, Dad, he's here. I've been at Darlene's and I'm fine. I'll be home soon, and I'll explain everything, I promise. Love you, Dad."

Marigold's eyes narrowed. "That guy who ran off was your friend Darlene's father, right? I don't like this. I wonder who he's calling right now. We need to get out of here, not stand around yakking. I'm calling the cops. And after that…"

"Oh no, don't," pleaded Laura. "What can we tell them? We don't know anything for sure. It's his word against mine and besides I don't want to get Darlene in trouble."

Lyle's couldn't believe this. They'd just rescued the girl from who knew what, and she'd had to grab the wheel to save his life, and Garth's. Then he understood. She simply didn't want to deal with it. She looked so tired, biting her lip and fidgeting with an embroidered bag that must be carrying whatever possessions she'd brought with her.

He wanted to be gentle. "Laura, he took your phone. And did he offer to take you home? No way. You get it now?" She nodded and Marigold was about to make the call to the station, but Lyle motioned her to hold off. He was still kind of woozy from passing out but...

"Marigold, you're right," he said. "Let's get out of here, like now. Garth, can you help her with those traction mats? I'd help but there's something I gotta do." He pulled out his phone and called Laura's number. He had no idea what he was going to say but then he remembered the fiasco with Sally Barnes's phone, the one he'd stolen and got caught because the cops had tracked it.

"Yeah, who's this?" Falconer had answered it, the fool.

"This is Lyle Prince who you tried to kill with your truck. Don't hang up. Are you ever stupid. You should have got rid of this phone right away, instead of which you've kept it, duh, and now you've answered my call. All of which the cops will get from the phone company. You are so screwed. Goodbye."

Garth turned to look at him. "Tell me why you did that."

"Because I wanted there to be a record that somebody had Laura's phone. It'll back up our story when we tell the cops what happened."

"Yes, but now you've got him even more riled up. Who knows what he'll do next?"

"Okay, so let's get going."

Garth and Marigold went to the car. Garth pulled the traction mats from the trunk and bent to help Marigold shove them under the wheels. She slipped and fell on her bum, cursing.

Lyle, frustrated by the leg, stood back with Laura. Her lovely face was so drawn and tear-stained that the impulse to hug her was impossible to resist. For a moment he thought she was going to push him off but then she melted into his arms, rested her head on his shoulder, and Lyle knew without a doubt that this was the most joyous moment of his life. He could have stood there holding her forever.

"Oh, Lyle," she whispered, "I'm so sorry, I haven't showered for two days. I have really bad armpit odour."

Lyle inhaled her warm scent. Nothing and nobody had ever smelled better.

"He was gonna run us down and you saved us," he whispered.

"Mm, hm," and a sniff, "and you saved me, too."

"So you wanna tell me what this is all about? The big mystery? Why you were here? 'Cos a lot of people, me included, have been," — he was going to say scared shitless but maybe not the best wording — "pretty worried about you, you know?"

"Alright," she said, her face next to his, so close that he could barely stop himself turning in for a kiss. She made a head movement toward Garth and Marigold. "should we tell them too?"

Lyle called them over and Laura told her story. The planned occupation at the cannery by a bunch of crazies, armed probably, how Darlene's dad was deep in it, how she'd found out and accepted an offer of refuge from Darlene and her mom. And there was this place they called *The Keep* where the crazies hung out.

The Keep, that barn again! It really *was* all connected the way Garth had thought. The part Lyle didn't buy was Laura needing to hide. That was a Darlene delusion, or worse.

"Well that was informative," Marigold said, brushing snow off her bum, "but c'mon already, let's get rolling before buddy up the road comes back. Garth, come help me unstick this baby. Gimme a push when I wave."

Lyle gave Laura what he hoped she'd see as a comforting squeeze and released her. He told her about how Hank Niles' death might be connected with *The Keep* and how the pathetic Southmead cops wanted to fit his mother up for it. The car starting interrupted his story. After a couple of tries, Marigold sawing at the wheel, it sashayed up the bank and onto the track.

All aboard. "Where to then, Lyle?" Marigold asked, "Home to Laura's?"

Laura, seated in back holding hands with Lyle, reached forward and gripped Marigold's arm. "No," she said. "I know where Lyle wants to go. Do you know where it is, Lyle? 'Cos I bet that's where Mr Falconer was taking me as well."

"All I know is it's a barn on Number 8 Side Road. There are two big silos by the turn-in, and not far from the Parsons Ravine."

Marigold twisted her head around and squinted at them. "You sure you want to do this? How do we know somebody won't be there? And what do you think you're going to find? It's too risky, guys."

Garth stabbed at his phone, checking Google Earth. "Miss Marigold," he said, "I really think we should go. We can at least drive by. Here it is. The address is 5122 Number 8 Side Road, fourteen minutes. Take a right at the next street, I'll call the turns."

The circuits in Garth's head definitely weren't stuck today. Nearly getting killed by a charging pickup would mess up most people, but Garth wasn't most people. From the look of him he could have just returned from walking

Ranger. Marigold shook her head in a display of — resignation? frustration? But she shifted into Drive and off they went.

15. MECHANICAL VIOLENCE

Marigold came up with a bottle of water. "Anybody?"

Lyle reached over, took it and offered it to Laura.

"Oh, yes please," she gasped, and took a long pull.

Lyle couldn't take his eyes off her as she drank. He was gasping too. In the previous quarter of an hour he had escaped death, then, unbelievably, held this awesome girl in his arms, immersed in the warmth of her. He hadn't felt so alive since, well, since ever. He took his turn to drink, putting his lips where hers had been, and Garth finished the bottle, presumably not too bothered about the health hazards of sharing after what had gone down minutes before.

"So Ms Marigold," Garth asked, "are we calling the cops now?"

Marigold drew a slow breath, then blew it out. "I dunno. You know I wanted to, but the more I think about it the less sense it makes. We all saw what happened but it's open to interpretation. Believe me, in my job I get to see all sorts. You wouldn't believe how people twist the facts. That guy would say we made it all up, three teenagers with overactive imaginations and a reporter looking for a story. Was Laura really being abducted? Absolutely not. He was planning to run down Lyle and Garth? Crazy talk! See what I mean?"

Laura piped up. "But he took my phone, and Lyle's call will prove it, won't it? Why would he do that unless he didn't want me calling anyone? And you should have seen his face when he shoved me in the truck. It was scary. He looked as if he was, like, on drugs, talking to himself." Her eyes had gone wide. "I mean, what was he going to do with me?"

Lyle put his arm across her shoulder, pulled her in and buried his face in her hair. "You're safe now," he whispered. Time stopped.

Garth broke the spell. "Okay, turn left here onto Number Eight Side Road, two minutes to destination."

This was not the most excellent section of the county. Farmland gone to scrub, swaybacked abandoned barns. In the summer, Lyle imagined, you'd see random platoons of scrawny, empty-eyed cattle. Isolated stands of pine stood to act as windbreaks. Two scabby-looking silos showed up ahead, close to the road.

Here it was, the place where everything came together. It held answers, Lyle was sure now, and seeing it for the first time brought a cold clutch to his belly. The barn stood beside an adjoining shed. A couple of crummy buildings nobody would take second look at, but they were exactly as he'd imagined.

Marigold slowed the car and they drove by. "Looks quiet," she said, "but what if there's somebody parked round the back?" Yeah, Lyle thought, the bad guys wouldn't park out front in full view. They motored on down the road, frozen slush crunching under the tires.

Garth was back on his phone. "Google Earth shows a space behind the barn, and a track that goes off into the fields. What do you want to do?"

"Is there a gate? I didn't notice," Marigold said.

'No gate."

Garth had it together today alright. He'd jumped in as navigator and mission control without missing a beat. And the way he'd stepped up beside Lyle in the face of that charging truck! The memory brought emotions Lyle couldn't name. Shit, he hadn't even thanked the guy.

Marigold swung the car into a three-point turn. Lyle silently begged her not to get stuck again. She didn't.

Garth kept calling the plays. "So will you drive in there and scoot out if there's somebody around?"

"That would be my plan. You all approve? Anybody not happy and we're out of here."

"Absolutely, let's do it," Laura replied. There was a set to her jaw. She seemed to have shaken off the morning's ordeal. The girl from the Mini Mart was on her way back.

Marigold's voice brought Lyle back as well. "And you, Lyle. You on board with this?"

"Me? Oh, uh, yeah. For sure."

Marigold turned in by the silos. The entry crossed over a ditch with a line of ice in the bottom, past a sign that read NO TRESPASSING. The track looked newly ploughed. A prickle of tension crawled between Lyle's shoulder blades. He remembered the *Brothers* game where you entered the ogre's cave and you knew, oh yes you knew, that sooner or later the ogre would jump out. Laura took a firm grip on his hand and he squeezed it back. Those radio waves were coming off her again.

Craning necks every which way, they turned beside the barn and came up on the shed. On closer inspection it was an equipment garage with an oversized up-and-over door, white siding needing a repaint, tin roof and an entry door beside the up-and-over. All quiet apart from a couple of crows picking at something on the ground. They gave dirty looks and flapped to observe from the roof. Marigold backed up to park, ready for a quick getaway. She killed the engine. They'd arrived.

Lyle pressed down on the door handle and took hold of his crutch. "I'll go check this place out."

Laura opened her door. "Well, I'm coming too."

"Hey, guys," said Garth, "don't I get to join in?" He didn't wait for an answer and exited the car along with Marigold. The four of them stood there, breath steaming in the chill of the bright, windless morning.

Not ten feet away was the door to the shed. No chance it would be open but Lyle hobbled over anyway and tried the handle. It didn't move. A window in the door was protected by a metal grille, fastened in place at each corner by blind bolts.

They walked over to scope out the barn. Two huge sliding doors were secured by padlocks, no easy entry there either. Garth voiced a question that Lyle would have preferred he hadn't.

"What's our plan if somebody shows up? Like, there's nowhere to run."

In that moment, the craziness of the whole scheme hit Lyle. How could he have let Laura, just rescued from one predicament, get drawn into this? He'd been riding a wave of selfish fixation on this place they called *The Keep*. He wanted to know its secrets and wreck the schemes cooked up here that had messed up his parents' lives. If he could burn the place to the ground right this minute, he would do it, but...

"Garth, you're right," he said, "we gotta go. Like Marigold told us, this is way too risky. C'mon everybody, back to the car. Laura, let's get you safe home."

"No, wait!" Laura stood in front of him like she had outside the Mini Mart. "This isn't only your personal affair, you know." Those cornflower blue eyes had him paralyzed. "This scheme with the canning plant, the reason I hid for two days in that gross trailer, this is their hangout, remember? So we get here and now you want us to run away? I don't think so!"

"No, I..."

This was hard to hear. He only wanted to get her out of reach of the slime bags who might...

Laura didn't pick up on his wounded feelings. "Guys," she said, "I know how we can get in there. I saw my dad do something once."

The sound of an approaching vehicle had everybody frozen where they stood. Marigold was first to move. "In the car, quick," she called. Too late, it was close now. Then it passed on by.

"See what I mean?" Lyle asked, "We can't be here."

Laura ignored him. She turned to Marigold. "The rental company gave you those traction mat thingies, you said. So is there, like, a safety kit in the trunk as well? Does it have a tow-rope?"

Marigold shrugged. "Let's go see." Back at the car she pulled out the fob and popped the trunk. "All the breakdown and safety stuff is in this black canvas pack." She unzipped it and pulled out a reflective safety triangle, a first-aid kit, a tire-inflation bottle, and a hank of substantial blue-and-white synthetic rope with snap-hooks on the ends.

"Alright then, Laura," Marigold asked, "what's with the rope? What did your dad do?"

The women had taken over, no question. Lyle waved Garth to stand back and let them have at it. Garth made a face.

Laura explained. "That grille over the window, we can pull it off. All we have to do is hook the rope to it and tie the other end to the car." She turned to Lyle and Garth, eyebrows raised. "Well?"

Lyle found himself stuck for an answer. The girl's readiness to commit mechanical violence had him seeing a new side to her. It was kind of, no other word for it, sexy.

"Sure, I guess," he mumbled, looking anywhere but at her.

"That's how my dad got us in the gate to our cottage after he lost the key."

"And then?"

"Oh, once the grille's off we can smash the window."

Rip the grille off? Smash the window? Was this Katniss Everdene he'd gotten hooked up with? He'd pictured himself as the heroic rescuer and Laura as the Disney princess. Not so much, dumbo. She was far ahead of him in her readiness to rip stuff up, and she'd called it right. What else were they going to do, stand around and stare at the door? Go Katniss.

Laura hooked the rope to the grille. Lyle tried to insert himself into the action by volunteering to crawl on the frozen ground and hook the other end to the car's undercarriage.

Garth stepped in. "Stand aside, dinkus. You a have seriously screwed up leg. I shall do it."

It took Garth a while groping under the car's rear end and Lyle was glad he'd taken over. Marigold mounted up. She eased ahead until the rope was taut, then, encouraged by thumbs-ups and arm-waving, hit the gas. The only result was spinning tires. The grille remained firmly attached to the window.

"Okay," Marigold called, "I'm gonna back up and take a run at it."

No tire spinning this time. The car lurched forward, the rope went tight with a sound like a bass-guitar string, and the whole door, grille still attached, flew off and slammed to the ground.

"Woo-hoo!" Lyle shouted.

"Yes!" Laura shrieked, and they slapped hands.

The place smelt of stale beer and cigarettes. To the left was a wall of cupboards. Two picnic tables were placed end to end on the concrete floor. A fridge hummed in a corner, so there was power. Next to the fridge and across from the cupboards stood a bar fashioned out of an old dark wood store counter, stools in front. A selection of girlie calendars decorated the wall behind.

A place to hang out, drink, and plan bad stuff. Garth was showing an interest in the calendar art. Surely he could have found plenty of that on the internet? Oh no, Monty would have blocked it. Garth saw Lyle watching and turned his attention to the cupboards.

A door gave onto the barn. It opened at a push on the handle. Laura, Marigold and Lyle went to take a look. It turned out as expected, a floor of tamped earth, a couple of snowmobiles and an ATV parked near the front doors next to a snow-plough blade.

Laura gazed upward. "You know, this place is really old," she said, "do they even build them out of wood anymore?"

The beams and frames were darkened by the passage of years but still bore the marks of the tools that had shaped them lifetimes ago. The age of the place reminded Lyle of his call with Dad. "Marigold," he asked, "what's a bootlegger?"

"Guys that smuggled booze, but where'd that question come from?"

"Because my…" Lyle nearly said *My dad* but caught himself, "my contact, told me there's a tunnel here, bootleggers used it. It goes down to the ravine."

"From here?"

"That's what he said."

They took a look around but found nothing that looked like the entrance to a tunnel. Then Laura called out, "Hey, come see this." She was pulling at a pile of tarps in a far corner. "Help me, guys, these are pretty heavy, but there's like, the edge of something here."

They managed to haul the tarps a couple of feet to one side.

"Well done, girl," said Marigold, "that sure looks like a big ol' trapdoor to me, but we can't waste precious time on it now."

Lyle wanted a closer look but investigation was cut short by a shout from Garth back in the shed. "Hello in there, come see what I found."

He had the cupboard doors open along the left side of the wall. "The locks on these things are of dubious quality. I found this and popped them right open." He brandished an impressively large flat-blade screwdriver.

"Let me draw your attention to Exhibit A," he said. The cupboard contained veterinary supplies, bottles and boxes with fine print on the labels. Garth had a package of disposable syringes in hand. He held his find out for inspection, gripping it by a corner. Each syringe was filled with a blueish liquid. The pack was labelled, "Razolam Large Animal Sedative."

Garth started to read out warnings and instructions about how to dose your sick horse by squirting it the animal's mouth. He was headed off on one of those obsessive sidetracks that Lyle would usually tolerate, but today he had no patience for it.

"Garth buddy, I'm sure this is real fascinating, but later, eh?"

Laura nudged his arm. "No, Lyle, shut up and listen. Go on, Garth."

Lyle shut up and Garth gave a nod of acknowledgement to Laura. "Administered in this manner, Razolam is indicated when a rapid sedative effect is desired and sedation by injection is not an option."

Lyle looked at Garth. "Yeah, so?"

Garth stared back. "Don't you get it? 'Course you do. *Not an option* as when you're putting it in somebody's drink, like Hank's, and they're going to drive off in a snowstorm? Injection would not be an option, I'm thinking."

Oh shit. Garth had nailed it, the annoying amazing smart ass. Lyle nodded slowly as his friend's conclusion sank in.

Garth wasn't done. "And notice, if you will, that there's one missing from this pack of six. Notice also that I still have my gloves on, so any prints on this package won't be mine."

Garth would make a mean detective one day. "Fantastic, Bruh, you did good." Telling Mom about this was going to be beyond special. He'd fetch her wine and a bowl of chips and, *Mom. I got news.* It would be awesome, mission accomplished.

"Marigold," Garth said, holding out the syringes, "can you place these back on the shelf for me and I'll get pictures." Marigold did as asked, Garth pulled out his phone, took a closeup, backed off. "Now one with you in it, perfect, and now one with you holding the pack." Garth had really thought this through. No way these pictures could be dismissed as fake.

"Great," Marigold told him, "now this is coming with us. She grasped the pack by the corner, the way Garth had done, and placed it in a side-pocket of her bag.

Laura was examining the contents of the next cupboard over. "Nothing much here, there's some kind of sleeveless jackets. They don't look like they'd keep you warm this time of year, though."

"Woah!" Marigold was doing her big-eyes thing again. "You don't know what those are? No, of course you don't. Those, young lady, are frickin' bullet-proof vests!"

This was beyond anything Lyle had foreseen. The guys planning the occupation expected to get *shot at?*

"Jesus Christ everybody," he said. "Come on, we got what we came for. Let's get going, like now."

The crunch of tires on frozen snow sounded through the open entrance. Engines fell silent. Doors latched open, slammed shut.

Lyle peeked out the doorway. A hulking black crew cab and an old red SUV with its tailgate open stood blocking Marigold's renter. Two men had their heads in the back of the SUV and a third stood facing the other way. The license plate on the crew cab read BIG1. Lyle dashed back to the others, pulled out his phone and thrust it at Laura. "Quick," he hissed, "get it outta sight." She gave him a puzzled look, but then she understood and shoved it inside her jacket and down the front of her T-shirt. Whoa, in her bra by the looks of it. Lyle couldn't help staring. Laura stared back. Footsteps approached the doorway

16. TRESPASSING?

No point in running or trying to hide. Three guys in ski-masks crowded in. Two carried baseball bats, the third, a weapon Lyle recognized from Dad's teachings as a pump-action shotgun, packing several shells. Ski-masks or not, build and dress had Lyle identifying them in about a second. It was Brad and Mitch from the Mini Mart, and Bert Falconer.

"You people are under arrest for trespassing and damaging property." The speaker was the one Lyle had pegged for Mitch Bigelow. Brad hadn't raised the shotgun yet.

Marigold's mouth twisted into a mocking grin. "Arrest? That's pretty funny, boys. You want us arrested? Call the cops. Go on, do it. No, wait, I got a better idea, I'll do it." She pulled out her phone.

In his head, Lyle screamed NO! This trio weren't the sharpest knives in the drawer. Who knew what they'd do when challenged? Mitch stepped forward. "We'll decide who gets called and when. You hand over the phone now, bitch, or I'll have to take it off you. Your choice."

Marigold, eyes blazing, held out the phone. She shook her head. "You people are in so much shit and you don't even know it."

"Oh yeah? What about you, sweetheart? Breaking and entering don't count for nuthin'?"

"Compared to abduction, breaking bail and attempted murder?" Marigold had figured out who they were too, then.

Mitch gave an impatient shake of the head. "No idea what you're talking about. We're wasting time here. You three, phones, now."

Garth started rocking back and forth, eyes down, making his humming noises.

Lyle stepped over. "Okay buddy, it's okay. Give me your phone now. It's in your pocket there, right? He patted Garth's jacket. Can I take it? Let me take it now buddy, it's gonna be alright." Garth nodded, eyes closed, still humming.

Lyle took the phone and held it out to the shotgun-toting Brad. "Here you go, dickweed, and before you ask for mine, don't have one, never did. Wanna check?" He put his hands up and looked Brad in the eye. Brad stepped forward, patted Lyle down with his free hand, shook his head. "What about the little hottie, shall I do her too?"

Lyle stepped in front of Laura. "Don't you touch her, you creepy shit."

Laura put her hand on his wrist and addressed Brad. "Somebody took my phone already, but something tells me you know that, don't you? So leave me alone, loser."

The poorly disguised Bert Falconer gave Brad an elbow. Brad backed off. "Got a mouth on her, don't she, for a doctor's daughter?"

"Shut up now, okay," Mitch said, shaping up to be the less brain-challenged of the Mitch and Brad duo. "You stay here and watch these while we step outside and figure this out." He headed through the doorless exit along with Bert.

Marigold parked herself at the picnic table. "You mind if we sit here while we wait?" Laura and Lyle sat, too. Marigold went to work on Brad. "You know you're facing jail time, don't you? What have these two told you? What is it about this occupation of yours that makes you go abducting people at gunpoint? Did you know the police have an alert out for this young woman?"

Brad's eyes went wide behind the window in the ski-mask. "How do you know about the occupation? And who called the cops?"

Marigold opened her hands and gave him a beats-me look. "I dunno who called. Maybe her parents. You think? It's on the news, you idiot. And when they catch you, which they will, they're going to lock you up for a very long time, like I told you already."

The guy's eyes were darting around and his pupils didn't look right. Lyle caught a gust of chemical-smelling body odour. An addict. Be careful.

Marigold kept at him. "And you out on bail from last week? Remember the conditions? Not to approach any of the witnesses? You really shit the bed this time, pal, and this only makes it worse. 'Cos yeah, Brad, you can lose the mask. We all know it's you. So be smart. Look after us now and we'll speak for you when the time comes. We will, I promise."

Brad yanked off the mask and flung it to the ground. Dull eyes, slack features, a rash on the jaw. The mouth worked like some dufus trying to figure out a math problem in class.

"Shut up now, okay? I don't need this." Brad started pacing, then walked to the doorway. "Guys," he yelled, "where are ya?"

No answer. Brad muttered something to himself. Laura twisted around and sat on the table-top next to where Lyle, still on the bench seat, was aware of the swell of her thigh next to his arm. Brad kept his eyes on her and she returned the stare. Go on Laura, Lyle thought, give him a hard time. You can do it. He nudged her thigh.

She picked up on it. "You want to know how we learned about the occupation? Well, I'll tell you. It was your pal Mr Falconer. His daughter Darlene found out. She's my friend and she told me. Then she begged me not to say anything. Stupid me." She turned to Lyle and rolled her eyes.

Brad's voice went squeaky high. "Jesus! Who else knows? Who the fuck did you tell?"

Lyle answered. "Nobody. Laura only told us. Well, probably nobody, unless bigmouth Darlene's been blabbing. Maybe she did, who knows? Could be the cops are on their way right now."

Brad started pacing and muttering again. Lyle locked eyes with Marigold. "Are you thinking what I'm thinking?" he mouthed. She nodded. "You do it," she whispered, "he's had enough of me."

Lyle stood. "Hey, Brad."

Brad spun around and raised the shotgun. "What now?"

"Here's your chance. Your buddies have gone missing, haven't they? Let us go now and you'll be the hero. No jail time. Tell them we made a run for it."

Too late. Voices approached the entrance. Bert and Mitch reappeared.

"What're you doing, man?" Mitch yelled, "Why'd ya take your fuckin' mask off?"

"They know who I am anyway, and that thing really messes with my psoriasis." He pronounced it *sorry-asses*.

Mitch threw up his hands and shook his head. He opened his mouth, but Brad cut him off. "Wait a minute, wait a minute! They know about the occupation. Bert's daughter found out and told the girl here."

Mitch, still masked, turned to face Bert. "Well, well. Look who couldn't keep his mouth shut." Bert didn't answer.

Taking his time, Mitch turned to Brad. "Listen, retard. They may have told you they recognized you, but that's all there was. Now they've seen your ugly face, this screws up everything. Don't you get that?"

Lyle didn't like this. These were the guys who had most likely offed Hank Niles by spiking his drink. So here he was, along with his little gang, in the hands of killers. Now he knew how reckless they'd been to come here. He could tell Laura saw it too. She had her hands clasped tight and he reached over and gripped them. Mitch and Bert moved away for another sidebar discussion. Lyle strained to hear but couldn't.

They came back pretty quick. "Brad," Mitch said, "you're screwed. You better collect your stuff and leave town, right now. Get in your piece of shit truck and disappear. Go see your old man in Kapuskasing or wherever the fuck he hangs out. We'll get your payout to you some way. Only chance, dude. We'll see to these here." The eyes in the ski-mask had Lyle thinking of something reptilian, a psycho, someone who would do unspeakable things to them and walk away laughing.

Brad raised the shotgun. "Oh, no, no. Forget that. You two stay right where you are. I leave town and guess who gets to be the fall guy? Good ol' Brad. And you two? 'Oh, nothing to do with us, officer. Two guys in ski-masks, you say? Could have been anybody'. And what are you gonna do with them anyway?" Brad waved the gun toward the captives.

"Well, that's none of your business anymore, is it? What you don't know can't hurt you. Or us. Get going."

Bert must have thought he saw an opportunity. He launched himself at Brad, a mistake. The shotgun went off with a mind-numbing wallop, the loudest sound Lyle had ever heard. Firework-smelling smoke filled the air and debris fluttered from the rafters. Bert dropped to his knees, hands shielding his head, apparently unhurt. Lyle hugged Laura who was making panting little sobs. Marigold tried to comfort Garth.

Brad pumped the slide on the gun, loading another shell. "Get going yourselves guys, I kinda like how this thing works. Go on, you're pissing me off. Beat it." Mitch and a wide-eyed Bert did what they were told and got out of there. An engine started and a vehicle moved out.

Lyle couldn't see how this left them any better off. They were captives to a nervy, gun toting lowlife who plainly had no idea what to do next. Marigold was still holding on to Garth and making soothing, shushing noises. It seemed to be working until Garth looked up, saw the shotgun, gave a whimper and buried his head in Marigold's shoulder again.

Marigold turned to Brad. "Stop waving that thing around will you? You're scaring him, can't you see? And you do realize, don't you, the first thing those two are gonna do is find a gas station, get on the payphone and call the cops.

Anonymous call, some crazy with a shotgun holding hostages. You're still screwed, Brad. You gotta let us go, like now."

Brad seemed to be considering the idea. Lyle decided to encourage him. "Yeah, come on Brad, here's your chance to be the good guy."

Brad wiped a hand across his mouth. "Uh, I don't think so. They're not gonna do that. You'd tell about the cops about the occupation. They're not that stupid."

He grinned, more of a grimace, "You think I'm some dumb redneck cracker, don't ya? Think you can wrap me around your finger? Yeah, I'll get you out of here, but not where you think."

He herded them into the barn, pointed the gun at Marigold. "You, stand there and don't move, you're coming with me. The rest of you over here. You'll be safe, maybe, if you behave."

"Where are you taking me?" Marigold protested. "What do you need me for?"

"Shut up, shut up now. Don't make it worse. You and me are gonna take a ride."

17. A KISS ON THE LIPS

Brad yanked the trapdoor open and motioned them down a ladder into a dark stone space like a small dungeon. Lyle was grateful for the support of Laura's arm. At the far end of the dungeon, the entrance of the tunnel gaped.

"Guys, you see it now, what a mess you've got yourselves into?" Brad said. "Me as well. You're gonna have to stay here while I find somewhere to put you. All I know is, this time tomorrow it'll all be over, but until then I gotta keep you out of sight."

"Remember what Marigold told you," Lyle said, "look after us and we'll speak up for you. 'Cos we're the closest things you've got to friends right now, Brad. You don't have to do this."

Brad grunted. "Look, I'm not like those assholes, okay? I'll be back." Lyle'd heard those words before. In some old movie?

The guy had a parting shot. "And don't even think of going down the tunnel. Don't try it. Believe me, you won't make it. Now watch your heads." The trapdoor shut with a thump followed by metallic scraping. The space smelled of decay, something rank. It was utterly dark.

Lyle grinned. Hiding the phone had been a game changer, they'd be out of here in no time. "Laura," he said, "can I have the phone?" She found his hand and passed it to him. He noticed the warmth from its cozy hiding place.

The screen lit up and cast a weak halo. It displayed the usual message *Searching for network*. The message kept on displaying. Come on, come on, stupid thing! After a minute, Lyle looked up, shoulders slumped. "Sorry, guys, no signal." They were here at Brad's mercy after all. He handed the phone back to Laura. She turned it off and darkness returned.

This was Brad's idea of keeping them safe? Lyle reached out to the walls. The space was barely two meters across and two meters high, the floor broken rock. It was really, really cold. They tried to shove the trapdoor open but it wouldn't move. Laura stayed quiet, apparently out of ideas for opening stubborn doors. Garth hadn't said a word since the shotgun went off.

Another Lyle screwup. Could he have done anything more stupid? He wanted to say something, anything, to accept responsibility for this mess, but he had nothing.

He heard Laura take a breath. "Come on, we better huddle for warmth 'til he comes back."

Lyle was okay with huddling, Garth included, but "Why did he take Marigold? Makes no sense."

"Doesn't have to. He's lost it. My dad talks about people like him. Everything looks different to them. What looks crazy to us makes sense in their version of the world. And he's on something. I could smell it."

"Yeah, but maybe he thinks she's like, his hostage?"

"Leave it, Lyle. There's no way to know what he thinks. She's smart, she'll be okay. How's your leg?"

"A bit sore, sitting on rocks, you know?"

"Try to keep moving, keep the circulation going."

Oh sure, try it yourself why don't you? But Lyle was absolutely not going to sit here, do nothing, and freeze. He didn't totally believe Brad's warning about the tunnel. He wasn't ready to open up about that yet though.

Minutes passed. Laura spoke. "So tell me Mr Lyle Prince, what are you gonna do when you grow up? Or if you want, I'll go first."

Lyle cringed, was this going to be like that Oprah show Mom watched?

"Okay," she said, "here's my teenage dream. I could be a writer. In English class Mr Hamilton has us write stories. There's competitions you can send them to. Living in Southmead you get ideas for stories every day, the weird people you meet, the crazy things they do…"

She went quiet then.

Garth broke the silence. Over his funk, by the sound of it. "Will we be in one of your stories?"

"Maybe. But we have to see what the ending will be, don't we? I like happy endings. Have you guys heard of Louis Sachar? I love his books. There's one called *Fuzzy Mud*, it's the greatest. The girl in it, I just want to be like her, she's so cool, so strong and smart. And she's nice. Makes me feel like I have such an easy life compared to her."

Lyle had to speak up. "Easy life? Are you kidding? Here in lovely Southmead, armpit of the county? And with all that's going on? You saved my life Laura, and Garth's, and when we get out of this…" He didn't know what to say next, so he said nothing.

More minutes passed in darkness. And it wasn't like nighttime at home when moonlight or the headlights of a passing car let you make out the dark shapes in your room. Here, for all the difference it made, you might as well be blind.

Once again it was Laura's voice that broke the silence. "What about you, Lyle? Where's Lyle Prince headed, a few years down the road?"

Oh great, she had to ask. Think! What could he come up and not sound like a complete dork? No way he'd ever be a doctor like her dad, or a lawyer, or any of those fancy jobs, much less a writer.

Then out of nowhere he knew what to say. "I guess I could be a cop. I look at the cops around here and I think, I dunno, I reckon I could do better than that bunch of clowns. And as long as there's guys like Brad and Mitch around, somebody has to take them down, stop them messing with people, don't they? Yeah, I could do that." And he meant it, he hadn't come up with it only to impress Laura. A flush of embarrassment heated his cheeks but she wouldn't see it in the dark.

"Right on, Lyle," she said. "you could do it. I mean, I've seen you in action. You should go for it."

His face was still burning when reality intruded. "Ah, actually, no. With my dad behind bars? I don't think so."

He heard Laura shift around to face him. "Lyle, you can't be thinking like that. Don't quit before you even try. That's not you. Look what you did to get my phone number."

Nobody asked Garth about his life ambitions and he didn't volunteer. They became a quiet group again, huddled together, shivering on the hard stones.

Brad wasn't coming back was he, the miserable son of a bitch? And why had he taken Marigold? And if Mitch and Bert had made the anonymous call despite Lyle's scepticism, the cops would have arrived by now. How long could the three of them survive in the frigid dark? Lyle remembered a news story about a guy who got locked overnight in an industrial freezer. He'd known he wouldn't make it, had written a goodbye note to his wife and kids. Well, Mom, he told her in his head, now you could have two dead sons. Monty would be on his own as well, and who'd walk Ranger? The last question ambushed him with a pang of regret. Ranger was a good dog.

Enough with the questions. Do something, anything. Lyle heard a sound he figured was Garth's teeth chattering. They couldn't just sit here and hope for the best, and the darkness was getting to him. "That's it," he said. "Come on, we have to go down this darn tunnel. We've got the phone for a flashlight, it's no use for anything else."

"Are you sure about this?" Laura asked. "He said he'd come back for us. And what about your leg?"

"Screw my leg. You wanna stay here and freeze to death? And we gotta get Garth out of here. Right, buddy? Getting kind of cold aren't you?" Garth didn't answer. He started making the humming sounds again. Lyle recognized the signs. They had to leave now.

"Alright buddy," he said, "c'mon, we're out of here. We're going exploring, it'll be fun." The humming only got louder. Lyle sensed his friend huddle closer to Laura and it confirmed what he'd feared. Garth wasn't going anywhere. Pushed harder, he'd curl into a ball the way he'd done during the pig episode. Trying to get him moving would be a waste of time.

He told Laura. "Please, will you take care of him? I'll go." Seconds went by and he could sense her reaching for her answer.

She found it. "I guess, but what's your plan? When you make it out to daylight down in this ravine, what then?"

"I'll call for help."

"Forget that. Using the phone as a flashlight kills the battery, and what if it runs out before you even get down there?

Here came the rising buzz of frustration again. What was he supposed to do? Anything had to be better than sitting here freezing, waiting on a jerk who was probably running. And anything to get out of this awful blackness.

"Look, I'm going, okay? And if I can't call, I'll hike out to the road and flag somebody down. Do you have a better idea?" Laura didn't. Lyle leaned across and patted Garth on the back where Laura held him. "We're gonna get you out of here buddy, okay? Hang in there for me, alright?" He didn't expect an answer and didn't get one.

Laura passed him the phone. "Hey, you," she whispered, "please be careful." Then her hand reached behind his head and, the last thing he expected in this god-forsaken hole, a quick firm kiss on the lips.

18. THE TUNNEL

Lyle left the crutch. The thing had been more hindrance than help and he couldn't see it being any use on the tunnel's rocky floor. His leg hurt but hey, he had the cast to support it. The phone's pale light worked fine. He'd spent what seemed like hours in pitch black, so it was plenty bright enough.

Needing to keep the damaged leg straight, Lyle braced himself with his right hand against the tunnel wall, the phone in his left. Turning his ankle on the uneven stones was impossible to avoid, and every few yards an electric pain shot up his shin. He stumbled on, tried to push the pain away and remember why he was doing this.

Why then? Was it about Laura? No longer was she simply a girl he had the hots for like every other horny kid in Grade 9. He'd rescued her, and in the same moment she'd grabbed the wheel of the truck and saved his life. She'd saved his ass at the Mini Mart too, and she thought he could be a cop.

When the two of them had hugged beside the track at Darlene's, he'd seen something he couldn't name in those eyes. In that moment he'd understood that while he ached to make out with her, he wanted to protect her too, be kind to her — what was that word he barely knew — *cherish*? Yeah, that was it, he wanted to cherish Laura MacDonald. The disturbing yet okay feeling made him scared of surrendering to exhaustion and pain. Come on, dummy, he told himself, think you're a badass? Okay badass, prove it. Do this for Laura, and Garth too. Or was he only trying to escape the darkness?

The pathway's slope got steeper. Icicles clung to the walls. Would there be bats? Spiders? Nah, in summer maybe but not now. Nothing could survive the cold down here. Each step was becoming a fight and doubts began to nag. Was he going to make it? Who would miss him if he didn't? Garth? Sure. Classmates at Southmead High? Not so much. Sandy, the school bus driver he'd been riding with forever? Maybe. He supposed Mom would, even though all she ever did was give him a hard time.

A voice in Lyle's head began talking to him. It sounded like one of Monty's lectures. *Lyle, are you surprised Mom's not the picture of joyful happiness? Think about it. Kenny died, then Dad went to jail. And what do you do but get in trouble and be a total pain in the ass? Now she might lose the store, where she goes every damn day so she can earn money to feed your face and keep a roof over your head.* Lyle wasn't totally filled with remorse at this. Okay, so why did it feel like she blamed him for everything? Then he remembered the evidence from the cupboard and what it meant for Mom, and he understood that he wasn't only doing this for Laura.

Thoughts about the women in his life were cut short by something Lyle hadn't reckoned with. The path became a stairway hacked out of the rock, crumbly and treacherous looking. How far down did it go? No way to tell, the steps faded into darkness beyond the feeble light from the phone. Nothing for it, start down, right leg first. *Shit no!* That hurt way too much and he nearly fell. Lyle flopped down on the top step, sweaty despite the cold, heart thumping in his chest.

Climb back up? His shaky limbs would never manage it. So, he was stuck, no way back and no way forward. Strangely this came as no surprise. The possibility, he now understood, had been lurking at the back of his mind, not waving its arms and drawing attention, waiting quietly for its moment.

Yep, another screwup and it was shaping up to be his last. He'd dodged death twice in the past twenty-four hours, but a third time? No way. They'd find him eventually, stiff and frozen, bury him in the churchyard with the old dead people. Or was there a kids' section? Maybe he'd end up next to Sally Wilson who got run over. He wouldn't have had much of a life anyway. Crap jobs, no money, no prospects. He'd tried his best but he was so tired. All Lyle wanted now was sleep. The memory of Hank Niles popped up, laid out in a drawer at the funeral home. Lyle wasn't so much scared as pissed off at giving up. He leaned back against the tunnel wall. His final thoughts as he closed his eyes were, "Bye, Laura, sorry, Mom."

But the broken rocky step tortured his behind, the leg throbbed, and his mind wouldn't settle. How would they be doing upstairs? He'd abandoned them and taken the only light they had. Laura and Garth were imprisoned up there in the dark. He'd been too keen to run, scared to hang in and wait, any excuse to grab the phone and escape the blackness. Well, the light on the phone still worked and shame hurt worse than his leg. Ah shit, he might as well keep going. But how to get down this godawful stairway? Oh, he had it now. Go down on his butt, arms and good leg doing the work.

He lost count somewhere around thirty steps. He was grateful for the elk hide gloves he'd lifted last year from Mom's store. They were saving his hands from getting wrecked as he lowered himself from one sharp-edged stair to the next. He stopped to rest and was close to giving up again when he remembered how Laura's lips had felt on his, and he forced his tired body to move on.

The steps ended. The floor appeared less steep and more even underfoot, gravel, no more rocks. Lyle staggered to his feet and fell into a semi-conscious repetitive shuffle. Right hand to the wall, left foot forward, right foot forward, repeat.

The air smelled different, fresher. On impulse Lyle turned off the phone and he could still see. Light, spooky light, coming out of nowhere yet it was there. Come on, he told himself, got to be close now. Green slimy stuff clung to the tunnel walls, the path turned a corner and daylight, real, actual daylight, beckoned. Unbelievably, he'd made it.

Lyle shambled out onto a ledge a couple of feet above the frozen creek. It was so bright out here! He flopped down against a rock and let his eyes adjust. The daylight and a stinging breeze jerked him alert big-time but any sense of triumph turned to anxiety as he fumbled for the phone, dropped it, picked it up, got it turned back on. *Searching for network* flashed up. Seconds passed, more seconds. It was doing it again, the piece of crap!

Then the *Connected* message displayed. But oh jeez, there was ten percent battery left, then it changed to nine. Quick, who to call? Lyle couldn't stand the idea of taking forever explaining himself to some skeptical cop. Monty, then? Laura's dad? No, none of the above because he knew who he was going to call, the person who would look out for him and never quit, even if she did think he was a little shitbag.

Mom picked up on the second ring. "Lyle, where are you? What's happening? I've got Laura's mother and Monty calling me and nobody knows what's going on . . ." Lyle cut her off. "Mom, I'm running out of battery, so listen up. I'm in the Parsons Ravine where the tunnel comes out from that barn. Dad told you about that place, right?"

"*What!*" What in hell are you doing there? My God, Lyle—" He cut her off again.

"Mom," he dearly wanted to tell her to STFU, but stopped himself, "please Mom, people could die so listen up. Laura and Garth are stuck under a trapdoor in the barn where the tunnel starts. They're gonna freeze pretty soon. You know where that is, right? Number 8 Sideroad, two big silos?"

His right arm, phone in hand, flopped down onto his leg. Dumb arm! Why had it done that? He hadn't told it to do that. He really needed to finish talking to Mom.

19. CHICKEN BROTH

Lyle's eyes were glued shut. No sensation of cold, no sensation of anything. He thought he was probably dead, and wondered, in a mildly curious way, how that was going to work out. Then warm breath touched his cheek. Could it be? Laura? He rubbed an eye open to be greeted by Ranger, panting dog breath and giving him doggy kisses. Which wasn't too bad at all.

Pushing through snow-covered clumps of dead grass came Mom and Sergeant Wowchuk. Somehow this was no surprise. Of course, she'd come. That was why he'd called her. But still, a surge of relief and gratitude enveloped him. Just for once, something in this asshole world had worked out the way it was supposed to.

Wowchuk carried a blanket. Mom took it, knelt beside Lyle and did her best to bundle him in it. She started rubbing his limbs through the blanket, then produced a thermos, poured the contents into the cup and held it to his lips. "Chicken broth. Drink." Lyle took a couple of sips. The warm liquid stung his cracked lips but it smelled and tasted fantastic.

He managed to swallow some more. "That's good Mom." She started talking, half to him, half to herself, in words of affection and encouragement, but also regret and self-blame. He didn't need that and mumbled lame stuff like, "It's okay, Mom, you found me, didn't you?"

Wowchuk was on his phone. "Yeah, he's here like his mother said. South bank of the Parsons Ravine, north of the road. You'll see my cruiser there. We're maybe five hundred metres in. It's rough going, mind. Okay then, be seein' ya." He moved out of earshot and started another call.

Ranger seemed keen to help. Encouraged by Mom, he laid himself on top of Lyle, a comforting presence but no light weight. Garth needed to cut back on the treats. Lyle put an arm across the dog. The low afternoon sun was on his face and he liked the feel of it. He hadn't tried to move yet and didn't plan to, but he couldn't feel his feet. Frostbite? You could lose toes. Hey, at least he wasn't dead.

"Mom," he croaked, "Ranger's here, so where's Monty?"

"Gone to the barn with Officer Leach to get Garth and Laura. He sent Ranger with me to find you. Can you talk? What in God's name is going on? What were you doing there in the first place?"

Lyle absolutely didn't want to get into it. The weight and warmth of Ranger were perfect. "Later, Mom. I'm kinda tired." He closed his eyes and let his head fall to one side.

"No, Lyle, no! You can't go to sleep." Mom's voice broke. "Don't you dare quit on me now!" She shook his arm and Ranger nuzzled around his mouth. Yuk. He wished they'd both leave him be, but then he recalled why he was here. He heard Wowchuk muttering into his phone and opened his eyes. The cop walked back and stood behind Mom, his face solemn. Judy turned to look up at him. "What?"

"Nobody there. They found this big trapdoor in the barn, open. Nothing. There's a Budget car in the yard. Leach checked and it was rented to a Marigold Wallace, that's the woman whose car got torched at the motel. So they were there, but they're gone."

Wowchuk regarded Lyle. "Sorry, kid," he said, "you gave it a helluva go. We'll find them but we need your help. So tell me, what in God's name is going on?"

Please, not again. Lyle closed his eyes and pretended to fade out. He heard Mom tell Wowchuk to back off and Ranger to be a good dog and lie down. A wave of despair rose up. Why, oh why, hadn't he seen what would happen? Stupid idiot, he should have stayed up there with them. Then, once Brad had come back, sooner or later there would have been an opportunity to phone for help. That was it for him. No more schemes. He needed to tell the story to people who knew their business. He opened his eyes and organized his thoughts.

The first thing to pop up in his memory was the vehicles he'd seen when he peeked around the barn door. The black crew cab BIG1 would have been Bigelow's, so the other one was Brad's.

"Sergeant, I'll get into it later but right now you gotta call in and say to be on the lookout for an old red SUV, like, a Bronco, the one they don't make anymore. 'Cos I bet that's the jerk that took them, Brad from the Mini Mart. He's the one put Garth and Laura and me in the tunnel. He took the reporter lady with him but he said he was gonna come back for us. I guess he did. Call it in and then I'll tell the rest of it." Or most of it.

Wowchuk made the call, then crouched down beside Lyle. "So?"

Lyle took slug of chicken broth and cleared his throat. "I managed to contact Laura McDonald, the girl who's gone missing. She told me she was at a friend's place and she said come get her. So we went and picked her up."

"Who's we?"

"The reporter lady, Ms Wallace, and my friend Garth and me."

"Did you know there was an alert out for this girl? You didn't think to call in?"

Lyle wasn't interested in pretending to be sorry. "Uh, no. I guess not."

"So what did you do instead that was so darned important?"

"We went to check out this barn on Number 8 Sideroad."

Wowchuk knitted his brows. "What? Why on Earth would you do that?"

"Because somebody told me it's a hangout for dirtbags, and I reckon Hank Niles was there right before he ran off the road and got himself killed. So Marigold, Ms Wallace that is, the reporter, she said she'd drive us."

The look of bewilderment persisted. "You still haven't told me why you went."

Did he have to spell it out for the guy?

Lyle spoke slowly, partly because he was dead tired and partly because that was how you explained stuff to a person with a mental age of, like, three. Actually no. Some three-year-olds were pretty darn smart.

"The ravine's not far from the barn. Seems like Hank Niles hung out with a bunch of sketchy people. So I reckon he was on his way home from there that night. I thought maybe they had a bust-up. Anyway, that's why we went."

Mom's expression hardened. "Lyle, are you saying I'm the cause of all this?"

Like he was trying to blame her? Yep, here she was, twisting stuff around again like always.

"No, Mom. I thought maybe we'd find something to get you off the hook over Hank getting dead. Like I told you, Garth and me figured he must have been at that place right before his crash."

"Aw, Lyle. Why did you have to go and do that? What was the point? You didn't find anything, did you? Now look what's happened."

Shit, now he'd have to tell, not save it for later like he'd planned. "Uh, Mom, we did find something. Garth found this pack of drugs for animals. Supposed to, like, knock out a horse. And the pack wasn't full. And they have a bar in there. Put that stuff in somebody's drink and then let 'em drive off into a snowstorm? I'd call that murder." He locked eyes with Wowchuk.

"Wouldn't you?"

The cop waved a hand like he didn't want to hear it. "That's a whole 'nother matter, under investigation already. Just tell me how you got put in that tunnel."

Lyle balled his fists. He sorely wanted to scream at this guy to get a life and do his job. He couldn't read the look on Mom's face. Disbelief? Confusion? Shock? Then she shook her head and Lyle got the message to leave it now, be cool and answer Wowchuk. He surprised himself and managed it.

"I told you already. It was Brad Watts that did it, the guy with the old red SUV. He must have followed us along with his buddy, Bigelow. We'd been there a while and then guys in ski-masks showed up, one with a shotgun. We had them pegged for Bigelow and Watts straight away."

Lyle wasn't going to let on about Laura's attempted abduction by Bert Falconer, for the same reason he hadn't told anybody about the permit-selling scam. Knowledge was power. He remembered where he'd learned that — Mr Musgrave's civics course. He'd only joined it because of Patricia Little — which had gone nowhere — and it turned out to be the only useful thing the course had taught. And right now, he needed whatever leverage he could grab, with friends taken and Mom in trouble.

"Brad took his mask off, so we knew for sure it was him. Then put us in the tunnel and took Marigold with him. That's it."

"Did he say anything?"

"All he said was he'd come back when he had somewhere else to put us."

Wowchuk had his disbelieving face on again. It reminded Lyle of a hack actor on CSI. "And you didn't think to ask where?"

"He had a shotgun pointed at us. So no, we didn't." Lyle'd had it with this guy. "Are we done?" he asked.

Wowchuk turned away and was getting back on his phone when two husky paramedics appeared, a guy and a woman, carrying a stretcher along the ravine.

20. GOING NOWHERE

Sleep was impossible as the ambulance bounced along snow-rutted back roads. Wowchuk led the way in his cruiser, light-bar on full outta-my-way setting.

At least Laura and Garth weren't stuck in the freezing blackness anymore. Lyle remembered how that felt and he couldn't help but be glad. But oh jeez, where were they now? A ridiculous suspicion surfaced but he pushed it aside. Surely Brad wasn't that stupid?

Other speculations took over. Mitch and Brad had been bailed out by Billy Niles after the Mini Mart. So they were his little helpers obviously. Well then, was Niles in on this whole business with the occupation at the processing plant Laura'd told them about? Yes, he had to be. But why would the head of the Farmers' Co-op be involved in such a crazy stunt? The only possible result was the end of the Co-op, couldn't he see that?

Shit yes, of course he could! But Niles chanting slogans and waving banners? Not in a million years. He must want the Co-op shut down for good. Which would mean the end of his job, so there had to be a big payoff off to make it happen, but from who? Lyle wished he knew more about how this stuff worked, but hey, he was pretty sure he'd worked out what Niles was up to. He didn't feel so dumb after all.

The ambulance bumped over the tracks, trundled into town and pulled up at the Health Centre. This was getting to be a habit, not one Lyle wanted to continue, thank you very much.

Dr McDonald and Monty were already there, summoned by a call from Wowchuk. Ranger, admitted under protest, courtesy of Nurse Jean, delivered tail wagging greetings to his owner but Monty had no time for it. Wowchuk showed his face for a minute, then took off to the station leaving Lyle, Mom, Ranger and the tight-lipped fathers of Garth and Laura.

Lyle was expecting to get yelled at but Doc MacDonald surprised him. "First things first," he said, "let's get you looked at." You had to give it to the old man. He must be busting a gut to grill him about Laura, but here he was asking about his leg like it was another day at the clinic. Except he had one eye twitching that wouldn't stop.

McDonald took Lyle's pulse and core temperature, a procedure requiring insertion of a thermometer in an unexpected place. That done, he stood back and cracked his knuckles. "Lyle," he said, "you've been lucky. No frostbite that I can see. Your temperature's on the low side but you're not hypothermic. What about that leg? How's it doing?"

"Dunno. It's still kinda numb."

"Hmm, let's see how it feels when you're warmed up some more."

MacDonald took a breath and looked across at Monty. Here it comes, Lyle thought. Good thing Mom was around because he had the distinct feeling that Laura and Garth's dads would pretty much have liked to strangle him.

"So Lyle," Monty said, "all we got from Wowchuk was you found Laura, then you lost her. You took off and left Laura and Garth to look out for themselves. What in Hell are we supposed to say to you. What are we supposed to think?"

Lyle decided it was time to tell the whole thing, the barn, Brad, the tunnel, how Laura had stayed behind to look after Garth. By the time he'd finished, he hoped they understood that his tunnel run with a bashed-up leg was meant to go for help, not simply run away. He wasn't sure they got the message. He wasn't even sure it was true, but they seemed to buy it.

Monty was shaking his head, his face a picture of anger and frustration. "What was that reporter thinking, taking these kids out to that place? Anything for a story I guess. Goddamn it!"

Mom nodded agreement. "I just don't get it. Some people."

Dr McDonald called to update his wife, a painful exchange to listen to. Then he and Monty got ready to head over to the station. Lyle was slated to stay at the Health Centre overnight, under observation, whatever that meant. Mom was leaving too, taking Ranger at Monty's request. Worry and distraction lined her face and she seemed glad of the dog's company. "Come on, boy," she said, "let's find you some dinner. Oh, Lyle, you want something? A burger from across the street?"

Great. Dog first, him after. Lyle replied with a thumbs-up. Mom exited with Ranger.

Was that it then? His part in this affair was done with? No way, be quick. "Uh, hello," he called to Monty and Dr MacDonald as they headed for the door, "there's something else, stuff I haven't told anybody. I guess I should have said before. I know why Laura hid. She told us. Just don't be any more mad at me."

The two parents exchanged looks, returned and took seats on the room's metal-tube-and-cracked-vinyl chairs.

Monty spoke first. "What now? There's more? D'you think this is some sort of game?"

"Come on Lyle, smarten up." Doc MacDonald said. "Quit fooling around, damn it. Tell us the whole story."

Yeah, guys, chill out. Lyle propped himself up on the gurney. "Laura told us about this gang of farmers. It's to do with the Co-op. Guess what they have planned for tonight?"

He told them about the occupation, how Laura'd heard about it from Darlene, got spooked and had hidden. Their faces told him he was in big trouble. Dr MacDonald slammed a fist against the wall. Monty's voice shook in disbelief and anger. "And you didn't think the Police needed to hear this?" He looked at Doc MacDonald who turned away and said nothing.

Lyle wasn't finished. "Guys, I know you hate me now, but listen to me. It's only a guess but think I might know where they are. What I think is, Brad has nowhere to hide them. And he's not too smart, this guy. So he'll take them along to the canning plant where his buddies are going to meet up."

Monty pulled out his phone. Lyle held up a hand.

"And before you call the station, think about it. From what Laura told us, this isn't only farmers. It's a bunch of crazies. Like, they have people showing up from all over, out of province, even. They call themselves militias, guys with guns. This won't be a nice peaceful sit-in. So then the cops show up, like, a SWAT team. Next thing is a hostage situation. Is that what you want? I got a better idea."

Lyle wished Mom was still here. Yeah, Mom, he thought, check this out. I've had it with being the weak-assed non-substitute for Kenny.

"So what exactly is your better idea, could we know?" Dr MacDonald's knuckles were white where he gripped the side-rail of the gurney.

Lyle didn't have anything you could call an actual plan. Just get to the canning plant, sneak in — somehow — and get Laura, Garth and Marigold out — somehow. Then he had an idea.

"We're running out of time," he said. "I need to call Billy Niles right now. He runs the Co-op and I bet he could get us in there. Can somebody get me the number?" That weird sense of calm had come back. He could see how it would play out, follow the plan that had formed in is mind. It would work. It had to.

Monty shook his head. "No damn way Lyle. You got Garth into this and now you want us to go along with some scheme involving that jumped-up bureaucrat Niles? Listen, Lyle, I know you mean well, but if it wasn't for you my son would be at home safe right now instead of…"

Dr MacDonald nodded. "Lyle, you're not going anywhere. You're going to leave it with us now."

Anger and frustration had Lyle clenching his jaw. Let the assholes of the world mess each other up, what did he care? That stuff meant nothing to him when it came on the news. But now here it was right here in his life, and those responsible would pay. Would they ever. And he was supposed to lie here like a pussy?

Forget being all respectful. "Guys, can't you see it? Yeah, I know, I'm only this kid from the wrong end of town but listen to me. I'm just scared that if a SWAT team shows up it could all…ah jeez, forget it." Right then Mom arrived with a burger, presented it to Lyle, and the three parents headed out the door. Adults never listened.

Burger consumed along with a Coke and fries, Lyle laid back on the lumpy Health Centre pillow. His leg started throbbing as it warmed up, but the peaceful quiet of the low-lighted room was pretty warm and peaceful…

He jumped awake. His watch told him he'd only slept ten minutes. He'd dreamed and the dreams lingered. In that short sleep, images of capture and abuse had returned to tumble through his mind. The SWAT Team would show up, cops in paramilitary gear, hyped to do violence. It could all go so wrong and here he was, stuck in the Health Centre, immobilized, out of it. No way. He had to contact Billy Niles. His phone was dead, so how? He buzzed nurse Jean and tried talking her into bringing him a phone. She proved uncooperative, got uptight and started treating him like a kid. "Lyle, no phones in here. That's the rule. I'm sorry."

She didn't sound sorry. Who made these stupid rules anyway?

"But I need to talk to Mom. Look, you've heard all about what's happening, right? People are missing, lives are at stake. Do you want people dead just 'cos you wouldn't let me have a phone?"

Jean pursed her lips but she stepped out and returned with a phone. The call Lyle was about to make would take every bit of smarts he could summon. Oh, one tiny problem, he didn't have Niles' number. No phone directory conveniently placed of course, no handy computer with the 411 website. But wait a minute, could you still dial 411 for a number, like he remembered Dad doing one time?

Nothing to lose, he hit 411. He was expecting the usual mind numbing *Dial one for this and two for something else and three to talk en francais.* Amazingly, an actual human being answered. Lyle gave Niles' name and approximate address. The operator offered to connect the number for three dollars fifty. He enthusiastically agreed, but then she said, "Oh, the number you're calling from is blocked from accepting charges." He was about to fling the phone against the wall when she added, "But you can charge another number if you would like." Nice of her to mention that. Lyle gave the Prince home number and the call started dialing. Push away thoughts of what was hanging on it. Pretend it was a game. Ha, ha. Funny joke. Niles might not even be there.

The call picked up. "Yeah, who's this?" Impatience and suspicion. This person really didn't want to be contacted. It was Niles, no need to ask.

"Mr Niles, this is Lyle Prince. Remember me from Court last week? Sure you do. So Mr Niles, I bet this is a pretty tense evening for you, right?"

Seconds passed. The response, when it came, was clipped. "What do you want?"

Got you, Lyle thought. Niles hadn't bothered to ask what was tense about the evening.

"Kid, are you recording this?"

If the guy had nothing to hide, why would he care? This was like dealing with a schoolyard nimrod like Troy Thomas, but then again, calling the Niles out, dissing him, wouldn't be smart. This had to feel like a dialogue between grown men. He tried to imagine how Dr MacDonald would talk to a patient, or Monty to a grieving spouse.

"No, Mr Niles, no recording. I know you wouldn't want that. Look, I'm calling to offer you a deal. I need something from you, and if we can work that out, the cops will never know anything about the occupation and who's behind it. You want me to go on?"

The answer should have been: *What are you talking about? What occupation?*

Instead, "Kid, you're full of shit. You have no proof of anything. All you've got is a few rumours and now you think you can shake me down for a nice little payoff? That's blackmail. I'm the one should be calling the cops."

Bluster and bullshit. Lyle was on a roll. "Mr Niles, I don't want money. I need a favour. See, your little buddy Brad Watts has totally screwed up. He's gone and abducted some friends of mine. One of them's that girl Laura MacDonald who disappeared. You still with me?"

"This is all so much crap, kid. It has nothing to do with me. What Brad does is none of my business."

Lyle had saved the best for last, but would it be enough? "Well, that's not quite true, is it? Like I said, I know about the occupation tonight. And I know you're in on it. Come on Mr Niles, let's get this done, can we?"

Lyle heard a sigh, then, "I have no idea what you're talking about. I admit nothing. But if I help you, these crazy accusations of yours, they never see the light of day, right?"

"That's right."

"How do I know that?"

"Because if I opened my mouth later, I'd be in trouble too. So here's what I want. Listen up."

21. SUNRISE, SUNSET

The Niles BMW sailed along Regional Road 28 in the twilight. The burger and Coke had given Lyle a boost, but the Coke made him burp.

Ahead, the sun had set. An angry crack of crimson layered the horizon but to the North the sky had turned dark and gusting winds were pushing the car around. Tiny snowflakes, the kind that meant business, began flying past the windshield. Lyle wasn't interested in the weather. Nor Niles apparently. Hardly surprising in view of their mission.

Time was running out. He had to get Laura and Garth out of there before it all went sideways. The plant came into view, the chimney a black finger flipping the bird at the evening sky. Lyle couldn't help asking, "You sure you can get us in?"

"Be quiet, kid. Get your head down."

Lyle guessed Niles didn't want whoever was manning the gate to know he had a passenger. He shoved himself off the seat and knelt, leg complaining again. Niles reached back, grabbed a coat and covered him. The car slowed, turned. A window purred down.

"Hey, Charlie, on duty early, I see. All set for tonight?"

And there it was. The fool had as good as admitted he knew what was going down.

"Bill, what are you doing here? You're not supposed to be here!"

"I know, Charlie, but no need for concern, my friend. I need a quick word with Brad, that's all. He's here by now, right?"

"Oh yeah," came the reply, "he got here at least an hour since. Drove right by me, never stopped. Went off round the back and that's the last I seen of him. Is there a problem?"

Lyle clenched a fist. Laura and Garth were here, he was certain now. But what about Marigold? Worries about her quickly dulled his sense of triumph.

"No problem Charlie, but I need to talk to him and then get out of here before it all starts, know what I mean?"

"You better hurry then. One lot rolled through Listowel ten minutes ago."

The Beemer moved off and Lyle clambered back up on the seat, intrigued and hyped. Here he was — and it seemed like a repeating theme — riding to rescue Laura. The woman definitely ought to quit with getting abducted. Then he felt bad for thinking that.

The plant loomed ahead, brick built, rows of small windows the way Lyle imagined an old-time prison might look. Not like Milton Pen where Dad was. That place, with its long low grey buildings and not a window anywhere, looked more like a car assembly plant than a jail. Except it had the most barbed wire Lyle had ever seen.

Niles drove down the left side of the building, passing a pile of skids and what looked like an incinerator. They turned again and, sure enough, Brad's old SUV stood by a shuttered loading dock. Niles parked next to it. In the gathering darkness, a light above the dock showed steps up to a side door. Lyle could hardly believe he was here.

*

At that moment, twenty klicks away in Southmead, Judy Prince was taking a call from Nora at the station. "I want to verify something." Nora said. "It's about Lyle."

Judy tensed. She had the warmth of Ranger's head in her lap, a carton of wine on the side table and, yeah, too bad, a joint. Lyle was safe at the Health Centre, so what now for Chrissake?"

"Ms Prince, I don't want to alarm you."

Like she wasn't alarmed already?

"Only, Jean called from the Health Centre. Lyle discharged himself. He got picked up by Billy Niles. They up and left while her back was turned. Niles insisted you'd okay'd it but after they took off like that, Jean wasn't happy and called me."

Judy fought to get a grip. "No, Nora, I was not aware. You mean she just let him walk out of there? Jesus Holy Christ!"

Nora switched to her law enforcement voice. "Roger that, understood. Your son taken by a third party without your consent. I need to hang up now and alert the uniforms. We're stretched thin here tonight, Ms Prince. There's some sort of ruckus about to go down over at Sunrise Foods, but that's not your problem. I'll keep you updated. We'll find him."

Judy had seen a change in Lyle over the past forty-eight hours. The Mini

Mart fracas, finding Laura, the tunnel, he'd been in the thick of it all. The expressionless-teenager look was still there, but…different, more focused. So where would he have gone, and with Billy Niles of all people? Well, that was a no-brainer. Where the ruckus was going down, of course. Judy called Monty and got voicemail. Nothing for it then. She killed the joint, threw on her parka and boots, shoved the side door open against piling snow and got in the truck.

22. ANOTHER KENNY MOMENT

The door at the top of the steps opened at a twist of the handle. Nobody around inside, dim lighting. The dock was a sizeable space with a high ceiling, random stacks of cartons and a workbench. "Uh, Mr Niles," Lyle asked, "do you know your way around here? Where could they be?"

Niles made a beats-me face. "It's a big building, there's dozens of places, if they're even here."

"At least give me an idea of the layout, could you?"

Niles blew out air. "Come on then." He led the way to an open arch at the back of the dock. It gave onto a wide gallery with metal-topped tables and sinks. A vinegary smell hung in the air. The size of this place! Oh jeez, you could search for hours and never find them. Lyle hadn't thought about that.

Niles pointed. "Off down there it's storage rooms for supplies, and past that are the offices. That way's the canning line."

Lyle started for the storage rooms, they sounded like a good place to hide prisoners. Maybe he'd get lucky. "I'll go through here, and you——"

At the sound of retreating footsteps Lyle turned around to see Niles scooting off back the way they'd come. He disappeared through the archway, the outer door slammed and right after that, an engine started. Goodbye and good riddance. The asshole was gone and he found himself relieved. Being around Niles had felt creepy. But was he stuck here now, like in the tunnel? No way back and no way forward. No map, no guide. Yep, another half-baked Lyle Prince adventure. Pain stabbed from his leg and he flopped down on the floor.

He had another Kenny moment. *Little brother. You got yourself into this. Nobody's here to help you, not me, not Mom, so smarten up and quit with the whining. Get off your ass and make some noise. Maybe they'll answer. You think?*

Get lost Kenny. You went and left us and now you want back in? It's not you anyway, you're dead. Good advice, though. Lyle hauled himself to his feet and headed for the storage area. A gangway, wide enough for two forklifts to pass, gave on open entrances to rooms containing racks filled with boxes. No closed doors, no prisoners.

He took Not-Kenny's advice and called out. "Guys, it's me, Lyle. Are you here?" If his shouts brought out a shotgun-toting Brad, so be it. But that could work too, Brad not being the sharpest tool in the shed.

He passed a suite of offices. The same dim lighting. Around a corner was a high-ceilinged space with skylights. A wall of discoloured brick stood to the left, and to the right a work area with industrial-size blenders on steel worktops. Handcarts stacked with blue plastic baskets stood alongside. He kept calling, "Laura, Garth, are you here? Where are you?"

Moving as best he could, and bitterly regretting, now more than ever, his mad impulse to beat the train, Lyle was approaching another archway when from behind him came a metallic sound. He'd heard it already today. The pump of a shotgun.

"Stand where you are. Don't move. Well, well, if it ain't Lyle Prince. What are you, my effin' stalker now?"

Lyle turned, nice and easy. Brad stood twenty feet away, tapping a foot and scratching at his face. Lyle eyeballed him. He had to grab the initiative, get the guy off balance. "Well, hi, Brad. So where's your pals Bert and Mitch? Ah, stupid me, I forgot, not your pals anymore, are they? Come on, Brad, you know you're screwed. You gotta get out of here like, now. My friends' parents are calling the cops, and if the cops see you waving that thing around, well, it'll be bye-bye Brad."

Brad stared upward, ran a hand over his head. "Come on, Brad," Lyle said do yourself a favour, get me to my friends and then take off. What else are you gonna do?"

"Why does everybody always take me for a fool? I let you all go and that'll be the end of it? I don't think so."

Somewhere, a ways off, a voice cried out. It could have been Laura's. The sound spurred Brad to action. "Okay, kid, head down this gangway here. Take it slow. And remember, I'm right behind you with my popgun, so don't get clever. You're going to join your buddies. Last thing I need is you wandering around loose. You're trouble."

Lyle almost felt sorry for Brad. Broken home probably, known to the law, schoolyard badass wannabe. Oh crap. He knew who else fit that description. But he wasn't that dumb. He didn't have to be another Brad.

You sure? an inner voice asked.

Yes, because the framework of his life had changed, upended beyond belief by Laura MacDonald with the red-gold hair.

He got moving, no problem taking it slow like Brad had told him, down a gangway past a row of giant steel kettles.

Heavy sounds, like big doors slamming, echoed far off in the plant. Ah jeez, they were too late, it was starting. Lyle stopped and turned to Brad who paused to listen as well. "Sounds like your occupation buddies arrived. You think they're gonna be happy you kidnapped my friends and brought them here?"

Brad didn't answer. He herded Lyle past a door marked Washrooms and along a passage to a space with the look of an annex or extension. He flipped on the lights, revealing walls of scabby whitish-painted cinder block. Skylights showed flying snow. Bulky items of abandoned and broken equipment were strewn about. A junk-room by the looks of it.

"Keep going," Brad told him. In the far wall, a robust door bore a faded skull-and-crossbones symbol and the words TOXIC MATERIALS! HAZMAT SUITS AND MASKS TO BE WORN. Brad dug in a pocket and brought out a key. Fuck, no! The idiot had put them *in there?* Brad caught his expression. "Ah, cool it. They don't use it for that anymore."

Oh, sure. Lyle remembered the scandal a couple of years back about a closed storage depot leaking chemicals into the creek. The stuff had a way of hanging around unnoticed until people, or in that case a bunch of cows, started getting sick. Brad slid the key into the lock and turned it. He shoved the door open. A smell like drain cleaner, or the degreasing fluid mom sold, hit Lyle's nostrils. Brad stood back. "Get in there."

Forget that. Lyle was here to release Garth and Laura, not join them. He got ready to fling himself at Brad but the guy had backed away too far, out of gun-grabbing reach. Run for it then? Hardly, with a messed-up leg.

Instead Lyle stood his ground, like he had in the lane at Darlene's, and folded his arms. Brad started jerking his head around, like he had neck spasms, then backed off some more.

A standoff. Lyle called out to the open door. "Stay there. Don't come out. Not safe here! Brad, I told you already, you're screwed. Don't be the fall guy. Get going!"

Brad wasn't getting the message. "Yeah, you listen to Lyle," he shouted, "keep your skinny asses in there."

"C'mon, Brad," Lyle said. "what are we doing here? The cops really are coming. They catch you here . . . with a shotgun? Think about it."

Brad let the shotgun droop. "Oh shit, they're going to arrest me."

"Shoot you, more like. Or maybe not," Lyle said. "Maybe you could be a hero. All you've gotta do is let us go."

"Yeah sure, like they'll give me medal, uh, huh."

"Could be. I'll vote for it, why not? I mean you haven't hurt anybody yet, have you?" Lyle wondered about Marigold.

"No, but…"

"And what's the alternative? Do you *want* to go out in a blaze of glory?"

"Fuck no," said Brad, and he took off at a run back the way they'd come, gun in hand.

23. STORM WARNING

So, this was victory, or at least liberation, and it felt so good.

"All clear everybody," Lyle called, "come on out."

Laura was first through the door, then Garth, followed by, no way, Marigold! Laura hesitated, eyes wide, then rushed into Lyle's arms. He hugged her tight, on top of the world yet troubled. They weren't home free yet.

"Omigod, Lyle, you're alive!" Her voice was all trembly. "You made it down the tunnel, didn't you, and now you're here!" She pushed away and looked him in the eyes. It made his knees go weak, like at the Mini Mart. "You saved me again, Lyle Prince," she said. The mischief was back on her face, like she was pretending to give him a hard time. "We need to stop seeing each other like this." Then the look collapsed and she pulled him in again and started making those little panting sobs. Garth stood by. Lyle wanted to hug him too, but they didn't do that, never had. Later perhaps.

"It's okay," he whispered. He patted Laura's back, like he'd seen adults do at funerals. "But how did Marigold get here?"

Laura sniffed and wiped a hand across her face. "All she said was Brad took her with him 'cos he thought she'd take us down the tunnel. They just drove around killing time for the Sunday shift to close at the plant."

Marigold had listened in. "And you were stuck in that awful hole. I had to make sure he'd come back for you like he promised."

"Did he…you know?"

"No, he didn't come on to me or try to fool with me, but he asked me all these pathetic questions, like where did I learn to speak English? The guy's a mess. Group homes probably, drugs. So I kept on at him to come back and finally he did. And guess what, when he opened up the trap door he didn't even realize you weren't there, Lyle! I tell you…" Marigold shook her head, then turned those big eyes on him. "So, Mister, the question our viewers want an answer to, how did you frickin' get in here for gosh sakes?"

She probably wouldn't have put it like that on TV. Lyle released Laura. He gave a brief account of his trip down the tunnel and events leading to his arrival here. Faces showed awe and thanks.

"What matters is you're not locked in there anymore," he said.

Nobody disagreed but Laura looked bothered. "So, where's my dad?"

"Last I saw of your dad, him and Garth's dad were headed to the Station House. But there's a storm starting so the roads'll be a mess and I heard a bunch of noise just now. Sounded like the occupation started."

"But the cops will get here sometime, won't they?"

"I suppose, but what are they gonna do, a few guys in a cruiser?"

Lyle could see the disappointment in her eyes. For some seconds the only sound was quiet breathing. Then he remembered another piece of not-so-good news. Brad still had Garth's and Marigold's phones with the pictures from the shed.

And to top it off, he still needed an answer to the question nagging at him. "So Brad came back for you after all, and me going down the tunnel was a total waste of time, yeah?"

Garth answered, evidently recovered from tunnel-funk. "My friend, do not be obtuse, if you hadn't got down there and called your mom, and then used your hitherto unrevealed superpowers to get in here, well." He spread his hands. "And—"

The sound of a loud-hailer, distant but distinct.

"This is Southmead Police, Southmead Police. Armed response officers attending. You are surrounded. Show yourselves, hands on heads, and you will not be harmed. To anyone being held under duress, stay in place and we will come for you."

The message was repeated two more times. That was quick, too soon for a SWAT team. This must be Leach and Jensen winging it. Lyle wasn't sure this was a smart move, but it meant rescue was only a matter of time now.

"Back in here then, I guess," Marigold said. "We need to do what the cops told us, and this is as safe as anywhere. Get inside and I'll tell you why." They trooped in and shut the door. The room wasn't too big, about the size of Mom's living room at home. A couple of armchairs stood in a corner — which was odd — and a worktop across the back wall displayed glassware, a sink and burners like those in the school's chem laboratory. The women got the chairs, the guys, the floor.

Marigold pointed to the apparatus. "Garth and I figured this out between us. Go on, Garth, tell them."

Garth frowned like he needed to concentrate. "What we have here is a meth lab. This," he lifted his eyes to the worktop and pointed to a jar of what looked like sugar, "is Sodium Hydroxide. And that's a can of Ethyl Ether." More cans and bottles stood on shelves.

Lyle hauled himself from the floor, took hold of the can, unscrewed the top and sniffed. Wow, major hospital smell! Cold and heady, it grabbed the front of his face. Man, you could get high on this stuff in about five seconds.

Garth spread his hands. "Dad uses it sometimes for, well, you know. Lyle, stop sniffing before it rots your brain. So here we have two primary ingredients of Methamphetamine, and everything you'd need to make it." He turned to Marigold.

"Yep," she said, "I concur. This is a nice little Meth shop. And it's no small-time home brew operation. You could make hundreds of hits every week here. See these?" She pointed to a box of Ziplock baggies. "And here's the packaging. Fifty bucks a pop. This is a helluva story!"

Forget the meth and the story. The Coke had found its way to Lyle's bladder. "I gotta go to the washroom," he said. "It's right back there, so no problem."

Marigold shook her head. "No Lyle, see that bucket under the sink? Use that. We had to. I bet Brad's still out there somewhere."

Enough with discussion of bathroom options. Pee in a bucket? In front of Laura? Absolutely not.

Lyle was about to wet his pants. He waved a hand and made his exit. The washroom was only a few steps past the other door. To his surprise the place had the fresh, astringent smell it was supposed to have. It was a small unisex facility with one urinal and a toilet stall, door closed. Lyle unzipped and let it go. He was enjoying the blessed relief when he heard movement close by.

He finished, shook off the drops and zipped up. The sound — a breath or a sigh, had come from the stall. Lyle busied himself washing his hands to buy time and get his head together. He dried them on the high-tech air blast thingy and came to a decision. "Hey, Brad," he asked, "that you?"

Silence, then, "Yeah."

"Still got the dumb gun?"

"Naw, I stashed it. You said to disappear so I have. I'm done with those guys and their stupid occupation. Now piss off and leave me be."

"I can do that. Nobody needs to know you're here. But you gotta do something for me. You still got those phones, don't you? Give, that's the deal."

Lyle moved to the exit door, ready to take off in case Brad came at him. He heard quiet movements. Hands searching pockets, then scraping noises on floor tiles. Two phones slid out under the door.

Another small, no, really huge, triumph. Don't gloat, he told himself, just get going. "Thanks Brad, I'm gone."

"You better be."

Fantastic! He had the precious pictures from The Keep. Back in the meth room, "Look what I got. Found them in the garbage pail in the washroom. Unbelievable!" He handed over the phones to Garth and Marigold.

Laura frowned. "You just happened to look in the garbage?"

"Sure, washed my hands, like I always do" — like, they were so not going to buy that — "went to pitch the paper towel and there they were. Brad must have dumped them. Didn't want to be caught with them I guess." He wasn't sure she totally believed him, but she didn't press it.

Marigold was already talking to Nora at the Station. "Yes, we're here. We heard your guys tell the occupiers to surrender and for us to stay put." Marigold listened to Nora's reply, then answered.

"We were locked in room, but Lyle came and found us. Can you believe it?" Another pause, then, "That's great news, I'll tell them…okay and I'll be sending you some pictures. Pretty interesting what we found here. Alright, yes, 'bye for now."

Lyle sat himself on the floor, his back against a wall. Garth remained standing and Marigold reclaimed her chair. "Nora said to keep our heads down and await rescue. There's reinforcements on the way and your parents too, Garth and Laura. Lyle, Nora spoke with your mom earlier. She's going to try her again. So we wait. We're safe."

An announcement, not a question. Cute, so who gave *her* the right? Who'd made all the calls so far? Good calls, too. Lyle was absolutely not happy to stick his backside on the floor and wait to be rescued. Typical play-it-safe garbage. Was that how Laura'd got liberated? Nope. Was that how they'd found the evidence to clear Mom? Nope.

He shook his head. "Guys, I have a real bad feeling about this. We should get out, like now, out the back way."

"And then what?" Marigold asked. "The occupation started and you told us yourself these are some crazy, dangerous guys. The cops are out front, more coming. We have to stay put. We're safe here."

Garth wanted to take a group selfie and with some reluctance Lyle complied, but the nagging need to make a run for it wouldn't leave him be.

24. NOT SHOTGUNS

Billy was out of here. He wasn't a taxi service. All the Prince kid had asked was get him in, nothing else. Serve him right for trying to bargain with adults.

He jumped in the Beemer, fumbling the starter button with his gloved hand and cursing in his anxiety to get away. Booting it along the back wall of the plant he took the corner too fast. The front wheels gripped but the rears let go and the car slid ass end first into a mountain of cleared snow.

Shit! Shit! Shit! Nothing for it but to dig his way out. Working with his shovel and placing the *Traction Thermoplastic Rubber Assist Mats*, purchased online, not from that bitch Judy Prince, took Billy twenty exhausting minutes — minutes he didn't have. Finally, breathless and beside himself, he got going, piloting the Beemer up the side of the plant. Snow still came down like the Apocalypse. He turned left at the corner toward the front entrance to be greeted by flashing blue and red lights. A hundred meters away stood a cruiser, blocking the gate to the road.

Much closer, at the plant's front door, were maybe twenty guys, several clad in snowsuits, the rest in camo jackets over coveralls. They stood hiding, sort of, behind a line of parked trucks. Two of the vehicles had snowplough blades mounted, nothing unusual in this part of the world.

Billy was trapped here, the one place he absolutely couldn't be found. No way to tell who was aboard the cruiser but he was pretty sure it was a Southmead car. A warning blared out from the cruiser's loudhailer. Wait a minute, armed response? Surrounded? By two guys in a cruiser, who were the dopes kidding? Reinforcements were bound to arrive soon though. What to do? Refuge inside the plant wasn't an option — they'd find him eventually.

Heads turned as Billy cut the engine and scrambled out of the car. The door of the plant hung open, smashed in by the looks of it. Low, agitated voices argued about what to do. Billy's stomach flipped at the sight of guns. Not shotguns or farmers' .303 varmint hunters, black assault rifles with magazines as long as a forearm.

It had all come apart. The cops were at the gate and the occupation was toast. Way more guys than this pathetic turnout had been promised but that wasn't going to happen now. Even as Billy watched, a pickup came by on the road, slowed, then took off at the sight of the cruiser's lights. Should he try to take charge? No, there were few faces he recognized, Charlie, one or two others. Most wore ski-masks, out-of-towners, self-styled libertarians, armed and bent on trouble. Two of them approached, one built like a bear, the other lean and tense like a weasel.

The weasel had a black rifle in the crook of his arm. He flicked away a butt. "And who the fuck are you?"

Think, quick. "Been checking 'round the back. All secure there, no problems."

"Well, no shit, buddy. We sure have a problem out front in case you didn't notice. Answer the question. Who are you? What're you doin' here in your fancy car?" The rifle twitched in Billy's direction. Goddamn McKaskell. Billy asked himself, for about the twentieth time tonight, how he'd managed to get sucked into this. And he wished a special curse on that smart-ass Prince kid.

Charlie Webb stepped over. "It's okay Wendell, I know him. Be cool, Bill. We're about to bust out of here. No choice, my friend. Wait up."

Every second, Billy expected to see a fleet of black vans roll in. Finally, voices hardened in the group by the trucks. Billy heard, "Yep, okay, I'm on it, let's roll." Two guys in ski-masks, one somehow familiar in posture and gait, grabbed long black holdalls from a pickup bed and headed inside. The holdalls looked familiar as well. Like the ones McKaskell had wanted delivered to Mitch Bigelow, courtesy of the trip that had ended Hank's life. Then he knew who the familiar figure was: Bigelow. What in hell was going on?

No time now for pointless speculation. People were mounting up. Doors slammed. Big diesels rumbled to life but nobody was moving yet. Billy jumped back in the car, frantic to be out of here.

The two men hustled out, minus the holdalls, and clambered aboard an idling Hummer. Snowploughs in the lead, Billy in the rear, the convoy headed for the gate. Billy wondered why the cops didn't jump out and start shooting. He continued to wonder as the lead truck shoved the cruiser aside with its blade. The follower finished the job and the cruiser, the worse for wear, landed on its side in the ditch. Southmead's finest were still aboard and keeping their heads down, the first intelligent thing they'd done tonight. The convoy streamed onto the road.

Something lit up Billy's peripheral vision. He twisted around to look. An ugly red and black fireball churned upward from the plant. The idiots must have planted some sort of firebomb. So here it was, the kind of catastrophe that had jolted him awake these past few nights.

Could he still stay clear? The odds had just gotten a whole lot worse. And so had the stakes if those kids were in there. Too bad, no way he was going to raise the alarm and come under suspicion for being anywhere near the place. Get a grip, he told himself, they'd find a way out, of course they would. But then, oh shit, they'd tell about Brad, and the fifty grand he'd borrowed to pay Brad's bail would be gone, just gone.

Billy struggled to push the panic down. After all, only one person besides the occupiers had any clue he was involved. Assuming the Prince kid survived the fire, there might be a way to shut him up.

25. THE TEAM

A heavy thump shook the walls. Little streams of dust dropped from the ceiling. Marigold jumped from her chair. "Mother of God, the fools have blown the place up."

Lyle scrambled to his feet along with Garth and Laura. He hobbled to the door and peered out. The junk room was dark, but snow whipping past the skylights glowed orange-red. "Yep, this place is burning. See? I told you. We should have got out of here when I said. Now come on, follow me."

Lyle got no push-back this time. He led them through the junk room, past the kettles and blenders, by the offices and through the archway to the dock. Marigold grabbed the handle to the door marked EXIT. It turned but the door wouldn't budge. She tried again. "It's jammed. Oh no! Is the fire, like, already stressing the building?"

Lyle peered around. The workbench offered hammers, wrenches, and a selection of power tools. "Chill out everybody," he said, "we'll get it open." He limped over, grabbed a hefty clawhammer and started whacking at the lock. The door handle broke off and rolled across the floor. Lyle stood back panting, flung the hammer away and swore.

"Surely there's another door?" Laura said.

"Yup, but there's a fire in the way now, isn't there?"

Garth held up a hand. "Lyle, wait. What this requires is a battering ram, like they employ on the cop shows."

"Well we don't have one do we," Lyle shouted: "so where does that get us, genius?"

The fire was announcing its presence with thumps, cracks, whistles. Not close yet, but distinct. He'd told the others to chill out, *so chill yourself, dude,* Lyle thought. He took a breath. Lyle Prince, this is the one time you cannot, absolutely cannot, screw up. He caught Garth's eye and made a head movement back the way they'd come. "You're right bro. Like you said, we need a battering ram." The two of them headed for the archway.

"Excuse me," Laura called, "you're taking off and leaving us? I don't think so. What's your plan? Where are you going?"

"Back to the junk room. Find something to bash the door open."

"No way, Lyle! What about the fire? Do you want to die?"

"No, do you? We'll make it. Let's go, Garth, quick."

Laura put her hands on her hips and tilted her head. "And we're just s'posed to hang here and wait for you big heroes to save us? Lyle Prince, if you're gonna be my boyfriend you have to stop with this. We're coming. Let's go!"

Her boyfriend? Yes!

They got as far the offices when the pain in Lyle's leg went nuts. He halted and groaned through gritted teeth.

Garth looked over his shoulder and turned back. "We are a team here. Don't go anywhere, not that you can. One minute and I shall return." He disappeared around the corner to the blender room. There came sounds of something, or things, clattering to the floor. Next, trundling wheels. Garth reappeared shoving a handcart minus the blue baskets. "Get on and try not to fall off. Can you manage that?"

Lyle could.

Onward past the blenders, Garth's driving at moments hair-raising — he nearly took out a junction box, which would have been sparky — along the passage to the junk room. The air carried a low, crackly rumble and an awful smell, like the time Mom had left the iron on Dad's shirt. Lyle looked up. The skylight was coated with snow but the fiery orange light from before shone brighter.

Garth, unperturbed, asked, "So what are we looking for, a chunk of metal?

"I guess. Something long and heavy, like a girder or some pipe." The plant had tons of piping. Surely there'd be pieces here?

They spread out, searching among derelict pumps, blowers, broken bits of conveyor. Lyle came across a length of I-beam. He could hardly move it, much less lift it.

The roar of the fire got louder, closer.

"Over here," Laura called, "this'll do it. Garth, bring the cart, come on!" Lyle found himself entirely optimistic. This was the girl who'd ripped the door off the shed, so of course she'd found something. The way she'd taken charge had him wowed, and relieved too. It wasn't all down to him anymore. They were going to be the most awesome dynamic duo.

Garth shoved the cart, Lyle back aboard, to where Laura stood with Marigold. They'd come up with a two-meter length of rusty metal pipe as thick as a person's thigh. Perfect, no need for discussion. The women hoisted it to Lyle on the cart. He clutched it tight, ready to get going. The scorching smell was really strong now. Sprinklers came on like an April downpour. The lights dimmed and flickered out, leaving only the hellish glow from the skylight.

"Ah Jesus," Marigold muttered, "how we gonna find our way back in the dark?

"The phones," Lyle shouted, "turn on the flashlights, quick. Let's go!"

The fire sounds had become a roll of approaching thunder accompanied by cracks, pops, groans of twisting metal—the sprinklers weren't helping. As they dashed past the blender room a percussive *whump* shook the air.

"Shit," Marigold shouted, "I bet that was the meth lab going up. C'mon, Garth, we gotta keep this cart moving!"

Right then the sprinklers quit and Lyle was glad. Cold water was running down his neck. They reached the dock and Garth rolled the cart to the exit door, Laura lending a hand. The deluge should have left her looking half drowned but it hadn't. Water ran down that angelic face but her jaw was set with purpose. Lyle pictured a warrior-princess on some rainy battlefield.

"Come on Marigold," she said, "you too Garth, let's get out of this effin" place. Lyle, give us the pipe. I'll get the front end, Marigold, you next, and Garth, can you grab hold back there?" They took the pipe and hauled it to the door.

Laura flexed her shoulders. "Okay team, we'll start swinging it. Ready? We'll go on three. Aaand…one, and two, and three!" Marigold slipped on the wet floor and fell on her behind. That's twice today, Lyle thought, she'll be sore tomorrow. The pipe bumped the door which stayed firmly closed. Garth looked back at Lyle and rolled his eyes.

A thunderous crash resounded from the gallery next door, the way they'd come minutes before. Smoke and sparks mushroomed through the archway. Stuck on the cart, a useless spectator, Lyle couldn't help himself, "Holy crap," he yelled, "the roof's let go in there. Come on guys, you gotta get this door open, like now!"

Laura ignored him and helped an apologetic Marigold to her feet. "Alright, that was just a practice. This time's for real. And…one, and two, and three." The pipe slammed into the door where the handle had been. It banged open and fresh air had never tasted better.

On the steps down from the dock, Lyle stumbled. Laura grabbed hold of his elbow.

"I gotcha," she said, "easy now, hold on to me."

Not a problem.

Brad's Bronco still stood by the dock. The storm kept coming. The plant burned. The four of them, Laura supporting Lyle, trudged through the snowy dark toward rescue.

The low honk of a fire truck sounded in the night, followed by the *whoop-whoop* of a police vehicle. As the survivors turned the corner to the front of the plant, Mom's Toyota slalomed through the gate, a fire truck on her tail laying on the horn.

26. KEEP YOUR MOUTH SHUT

First thing, still dark out, Lyle heard Mom push through the door of his room. She perched on the foot of his bed in her housecoat, displacing Diesel who stalked off with a backward stare. Lyle put his head under the covers. It wasn't going to work though.

"Lyle, I need to ask you a question," his mother said.

Uh, oh. Mom Conference coming up. Lyle started organizing his headspace. He started replaying the events of last night, following the escape.

Chief Harrington had shown up outside the fiercely burning plant. None too soon. There was chaos all around and The Chief was barely coping. He had a banged-up cruiser in the ditch and two shamefaced officers to deal with. The firemen were having a teeny-weeny problem with a frozen hydrant that wasn't supposed to freeze. Mom, Monty and Doc MacDonald had already arrived.

Harrington huddled everyone under a tarp and cut to the chase. "Folks, I think I have the big picture. We'll be on the lookout for Watts and Bigelow, but this is not the time or place for statements. Can I see you all at the Station at ten tomorrow? Nobody's in trouble but I need your stories. Bring lawyers if you want."

Lyle stretched and yawned. Booting up his brain was taking a while like the school's crappy laptop. "Mom, could I at least get, like, some orange juice?" He had no memory of dreams or night thoughts. He must have slept deep. Orange juice supplied, the Mom Conference got under way.

"Lyle, just tell me, then I have to clear the drive so we can get going. Billy Niles called last night. He owns my store now Hank's gone. He said he wouldn't kick me out if you'd keep your mouth shut. Something about this whole mess at Sunrise."

Lyle came wide awake in a hurry. Keep his mouth shut about what? The permit-selling shakedown? No, it had to be Niles' hand in the occupation that Lyle'd used to blackmail him for a ride to the plant. And while it was all guesswork, Niles had gone for it, Charlie the guy on the gate had pretty much confirmed it, and now Niles was arm-twisting Mom over it. Case closed, it was true. He told Mom.

"But Mom, there's no proof the cops would look at. He'd say it was some kid making stuff up." It took Lyle barely a moment to decide. "But sure, Mom, you bet I'll zip it. And you get to keep the store? Awesome!" He remembered something else he had to tell her, more good news.

Mom got there first but she sounded scared to ask. "Lyle, what was it you said to Wowchuk, down in the ravine, about a pack of syringes in that shed?"

Lyle described Garth's discovery of the knockout mixture in the cupboard. "And Marigold took it, so there's no chance of them making it disappear. I dunno Mom, but I bet that's enough to get them wondering if Hank got drugged and you had nothing to do with it."

"But if it's not there anymore the cops won't want to believe you, will they? You should have left it for them to find. Now it's just your word you found it."

"Uh, no Mom, we have pictures. Garth took them on his phone. The syringes, right there on the shelf."

Mom went quiet. She stared down at the counterpane. Diesel padded back in licking his chops, jumped up and started head-rubbing against her sleeve. She pushed him off, palmed a tissue, and dabbed her eyes. "And that's why you went out there, wasn't it, you dear, silly boy? To help me."

Lyle had no idea what to say or do but then he remembered. He put his arms around his mother and patted her back like he had with Laura in the junk room.

27. A DAY OF FIRSTS

Waffles and sausages slathered in Maple syrup were Lyle's all-time premier breakfast. The snowblower droned out front. From the rise and fall of its engine note, Lyle could tell Mom was having a hard time boring through the wall of snow the plough had shoved across the drive. Twice she stalled it. Snow clearing supposed to be his job and wished he was up for it like usual. He poured a final glug of syrup on the remains of the last waffle, scarfed it down, shuffled over and jammed his plate and cutlery in the dishwasher. That was a first. This might be a day of firsts.

Mom came in, brushing snow off her jeans. She chugged the last of the coffee and turned off the machine. "Come on you," she said, "let's go."

Snowbanks along Mary Street dazzled in the low sun of another freezing morning. In town, shopkeepers wielded shovels and scattered snow melter. The place had a sense of lively purpose, people getting on with business after the storm.

A TV van had parked by the War Memorial. A woman with big hair and a microphone stood talking to a camera. They hadn't wasted any time.

Curiosity, scary anticipation. Lyle asked himself if yesterday's connection with Laura was for real. Or was he headed back to being the sketchy kid she had no time for? He didn't think so but yesterday was one day. He'd find out pretty soon.

It got crowded fast in the Station parking lot, out back where the booze trucks had unloaded in more prosperous times. The MacDonalds arrived in their Volvo crossover, Garth and Monty in a huge funereal black classic Lincoln which Garth had christened *The Aircraft Carrier*, Mom and Lyle in the truck, and Marigold in her anonymous renter.

The sight of a silver BMW had Lyle doing a double take. Oh great, what was he doing here? Well, not too hard to figure. Niles would have expected this meeting, known his name would come up, so he'd decided to run interference. The car door opened. The owner emerged and approached Judy and Lyle. The rest of the party looked on with a mix of curiosity and concern.

Judy waved them to keep going like this was no big deal. Billy held out a legal-size brown envelope.

"Ms Prince, per our conversation. Here's your lease, all signed off. Check it if you want. Do we have a deal?"

Look at the sour expression on him. Lyle despised the jerk beyond belief but checking the document was hardly necessary. Niles would be falling over himself to lock in the arrangement before Mom changed her mind.

Mom obviously figured the same and took the envelope. "Thank you. Yes we have a deal. Come on Lyle." Envelope in hand, she turned to follow the others. Niles shrugged like he'd expected nothing else and headed to his car.

Greeted with a nod by Officer Jensen on a smoke break by the back door, everybody trooped inside and down a hallway to Reception, where worn paintwork and a corkboard covered in notices about wanted felons and road closures served as decor. Nora took them through to the conference room. No windows, a hardwood table, leatherette upholstered chairs and a portrait of The Queen on the far wall. No sign of The Chief yet. After a minute, Marigold got up and came over to where Lyle sat with Mom. "Ms Prince, do you mind if I step outside with your son for a moment? I need to ask him something."

Bad idea Marigold. Mom would have no time for this after she'd learned how the reporter had taken him to *The Keep*. Lyle steeled himself for the outburst but Mom opened her hands. "Sure, go ahead." She leaned back in her chair and shut her eyes. She's exhausted, he thought.

Garth, sitting beside his father, did his eye-rolling thing, the corners of his mouth turned down. Oh come on, did he really see Laura and Marigold as competition, a threat to their friendship? What a dope.

In the hallway, "So Lyle, what's going on?" Marigold asked.

He took a moment. "This is only me guessing, alright?"

"Doesn't matter, guess away."

"Well, I reckon Niles knew about the occupation from the start, in fact I think he put them up to it. He wants the Co-op shut down and he'll get a big payoff from somebody. Who that is, I dunno."

Marigold frowned. "Where exactly is this coming from, if you don't mind my asking?"

A moment ago she'd wanted his take on it all, now she thought he'd made it up? Whatever. Lyle repeated the explanation he'd given Mom, how he'd arm-twisted Niles, how Charlie on the gate had pretty much confirmed Niles was involved when he'd greeted him.

"Oh wow," Marigold said, not so sceptical anymore, "you really have been figuring this out, haven't you? What else?"

"So if Niles is getting a kickback for getting the Co-op shut down, wouldn't that be from whoever owns the plant, because wouldn't they hate the Co-op for keeping the farmer's prices up? I bet Mitch Bigelow'd know. He's in this up to his scrawny neck."

She shook her head. "No need to ask anybody. See, there's this guy McKaskell, boss of Sunrise Foods, a real sweetheart. Lawsuits all the time, contract violations, you name it, but he always weasels out of it. Why Mitch Bigelow, anyway? What would *he* know?"

Lyle reminded her about the permit extortion, how Mitch was the collecting agent for Niles. She rubbed her chin, thinking, excited, a reporter smelling a career-building story. "So how do I find this Mitch Bigelow person? He's the one with the buzzcut and the tattoos, right? Got any idea where he hangs out?"

"No, but I know who might. His name's Lee Wowchuk. He's the sergeant's kid but they're, like, estranged. He lives in a trailer park out on the Woodchester Road. Has an old Airstream, silver, and a van, sorta grey, and a skidoo. Rides a Harley in the summer."

"How do you know him?" Then Marigold backed off like she suspected he'd rather not say. "Doesn't matter, leave it with me."

Chief Harrington and Sergeant Wowchuk stepped out of a door down the hall and ushered Lyle and Marigold back to join the others in the conference room. Everybody sat and the Chief got right to it. "Folks, here's my problem. My boss wants answers like, yesterday, so I need your help to piece this thing together quick or the OPP will come marching in here and turn it into a circus. Nobody wants that, do they, so let's see if we can deal with it here in Southmead."

"Ms Wallace, I need a favour from you. Can you give me twenty-four hours before any of this hits *The Beacon?* I mean, report the fire and all, but not the rest of it?"

Marigold pulled a face. "Well, Chief, I guess I can do that, but twenty-four hours, no more, okay? I can sell my editor on it, just so long as there's no stories popping up from *Sources that asked not to be named.* Are we good?"

"We're good."

Wouldn't this be huge for Marigold? Breaking a story like this could get her the promotion she was after.

"Chief," she said, "can I ask a favour in return? I need to step out. I'll be back, promise."

Harrington waved a hand. "No problem. Now then, Ms Prince and Lyle, follow me please."

Oh, so this wasn't going to be a group session. Lyle should have expected this. Harrington would be looking for inconsistencies, catch somebody spinning a story.

The interview room didn't have the one-way mirror or chairs screwed to the floor like on the cop shows. It was a plain, windowless room with shiny grey painted walls. Lyle and Mom took hard chairs facing Harrington and Wowchuk across an Arborite-topped table on which sat the one item the TV shows did have, a recorder. Harrington made no move to turn it on. He smoothed his moustache with an index finger and thumb and leaned forward.

"Ms Prince, before we get to last night, I have some news I think you'll be happy to hear. We've concluded that we were barking up the wrong tree regarding the Hank Niles situation."

Situation? Hank had enough dope to knock out a horse slipped in his drink, wiped out in his car and died, and that was *a situation*?

"The autopsy results came back on Mr Niles. Lyle, my Sergeant here mentioned what you told him in the ravine, about the animal sedative with a fancy name he couldn't remember. So I asked Kincardine to check. We got the answer yesterday. Long story short, yes he was drugged with that stuff. And Lyle, do I hear you have pictures?"

"Not me. Garth has them on his phone. You want them, right?"

"If you please. And better yet, we have physical evidence. Ms Wallace passed over the syringes last night as you were leaving. She told me how she pulled them off the shelf. Can you confirm you saw her do that?"

"Absolutely." Wow, the morning was turning out pretty good. Mom keeping her store and in the clear over Hank Niles, all in the same day? Better than winning the lottery.

"Excellent. So like I said, Ms Prince, we will not be pursuing you as involved. I think you better give your son a very big hug."

No hug, but Mom reached over and squeezed Lyle's hand. He put his other hand over hers and squeezed back. Another first today. Huh, so Wowchuk had passed along his suspicions. And they'd been acted on. Quite the surprise, maybe the cops in this town weren't totally dumb after all.

Harrington started the recorder and went through the routine of saying who was here, the time and place.

"Lyle, let's go back to yesterday morning and start from there."

Lyle told his story, starting with texting Laura, picking her up at Darlene's, why she'd hidden there, heading to the *The Keep*, getting abducted.

Harrington told him to fast-forward. He'd already heard about the tunnel episode from Wowchuk. Lyle described getting a ride to the Sunrise Plant from Niles, about running into Brad, about the meth lab and escaping the jaws of the fire.

Mention of the meth lab had Harrington scribbling on a notepad. "Yeah, we got the pictures Ms Wallace took. Good thing too, because there won't be much left to see now."

The Chief put down his ballpoint. "Okay, back up. You say you twisted Mr Niles' arm to take you out there, and you told him about the occupation, and about Brad Watts abducting your friends. Did he sound surprised?"

"Not as surprised as he should have been, maybe he knew something. Why don't you ask him?"

"Oh I already have. But that's all there was? Didn't he want to know where you got your information?"

"Yes, but I wasn't gonna tell him, was I?"

"See Lyle, he tells a different story. He says once you told him about your friends being abducted he was only too pleased to be a Good Samaritan and help. He says Brad Watts is no friend of his."

"Are you kidding me?" Lyle blurted out. "Niles forked over a ton of bail money for Brad just last week. You were there, Chief!"

Harrington gave a barely perceptible nod and turned off the recorder. "Alright Lyle, I'm curious. You have a look in your eye that tells me you think you have this whole thing figured out. Want to tell me?"

Harrington wanted his take on this business too? First, Marigold, now the Chief?

Lyle looked over at his mother. He decided to dish the dirt on Niles. Mom had her lease after all and he felt not a shred of guilt at the prospect. Mom hesitated, frowned, and a look of resignation, defeat almost, crossed her face. Then it passed. "Go on Lyle," she said, "tell him all of it, the whole thing. But Chief, this is off the record, right? Don't get my son in trouble."

Harrington pointed to the recorder. "As you see. Go ahead, Lyle."

Lyle repeated his guesses about Niles' hand in the occupation. "And you know who you might want to ask about all this, if you ever find him? Mitch Bigelow."

He started to tell Harrington about the permit-selling shakedown. The Chief held up his hand.

"That's old news, never proven. Is that all you got?"

"No. Who d'you think was selling the meth? Bigelow I bet, on his trips around the county." He'd have found a ready market. It was common knowledge how life on the farm could send you mental, especially in winter with the swish of wind turbines the only soundtrack.

Lyle could tell the Chief was buying into his theories. Something else occurred to him. "And burning the place down got rid of the meth lab didn't it? I bet the whole thing was getting too risky."

Harrington gave a smoker's raspy chuckle. "Ooh, yeah. Risky ain't the half of it. Meth labs go up like fireworks all the time. You people were sitting in a bomb factory there."

Too right, they'd heard it blow. Lyle's brain kept kicking stuff out, like he couldn't stop it. "And when you catch Bigelow, check his prints against that pack of syringes from the shed."

Harrington's eyes went a little wider. "Will do, I like the way you think."

Meeting adjourned, Harrington thanked them. "I'll be in touch. Lyle, you did good yesterday and I appreciate you sharing your thoughts. Would you mind asking the rest of them to come in now?"

Back in the conference room, the Chief's invitation delivered, Garth and Laura, along with their parents, got to their feet. Doc MacDonald asked how the interrogation had gone.

"Awesome," Lyle replied, "all good." He caught Laura's eye and gave a thumbs-up. She beamed back at him.

Doc MacDonald paused at the door. "Can you wait for us? There's something else we need to talk about."

Mom raised an eyebrow, "Like what?"

"Ms Prince, bear with me. We'll be back quick as we can."

"I hope so, I'm expecting deliveries."

Laura followed her father to the door. She brushed past Lyle, close, gave his arm a squeeze and off they went, along with Garth and his dad, for their interview with the Chief. Lyle wondered what Laura's parents might be thinking about their daughter and this kid from the wrong side of the tracks getting friendly.

Mom and Lyle sat alone together in the conference room. "Damn Doctors," she muttered, "think you're at their beck and call. Should be the other way around."

"Aw, Mom, lighten up. Look what just happened. The cops finally got the message about Hank's accident." Awesome hardly covered it.

Mom went quiet. She gave a puzzled shake of the head, like she'd just noticed something that had been staring her in the face. "Lyle, you've grown up and I've been looking the other way. Dad would be so proud of you, what you've done. He's not here and now you've stepped up and looked after me, and…"

"Mom, don't beat yourself up. You hoped I'd be Kenny's replacement and I let you down. You were always on my case and I deserved it, and I know why, because I've been wanting to still be a kid and just mess around. I didn't want to be Kenny. I get it, Mom, I do."

Mom hugged him for a long time, which was okay, except he was starting to wonder where Marigold had got to.

28. HOW TO THANK YOU

Marigold drove past the trailer park. All quiet. Fifty meters down the road she stopped, turned, and motored back to the entrance. A laneway was lined with trailers either side, maybe forty in all. The compound backed up against a woodlot, the trees brown and bare, snow in the branches. Marigold recalled a drug bust in place like this a couple of months back, a refuge for a mix of sketchy people and golden agers low on cash.

Halfway down on the left she picked out the silver Airstream, old but with the unmistakable rounded-off shape. There was no gate, no guard post — not that kind of place. A faded sign on a pole read *Valley View Mobile Home Park. Private Road.* She turned in, driving slowly. The promised grey van stood beside the Airstream, next to it a lumpy shape under a tarp, the skidoo.

Marigold found herself gripped by doubt. Wowchuk Junior was a biker, Lyle'd said, moved in the same circles as Bigelow, lived in a retro-icon trailer. A profile formed. Badass with a pigtail, into rock and roll and strip bars. Heavyset like his father and a gut on him. Did she really want to march up, knock on the door and ask this person where Bigelow lived? That wasn't likely to go down well. Could she make up a story, Bigelow had won the lottery and she needed to find him? As if. She crawled on by, wondering about her next move.

A white-haired gentleman, snow-pusher in hand, waved her down. She dropped the window. Watery blue eyes studied her and his cheeks bore an unhealthy flush.

"Can I help you?" More a challenge than an offer of assistance. This would be the self-appointed local custodian and busybody. Reporters learned to recognize these people in an instant. You wanted the dirt? They'd have it. But not today, she decided. Brush the guy off with a bogus question. "Do you have a James Wallace — her dad's name — living here?"

"Do you know him?"

"He's a relative. It's been a while."

"Sorry, Miss. No James Wallace here, no coloured people at all."

Yeah, really, she thought, and you're totally fine with that, aren't you? She faked a smile. "Thank you then. Wrong trailer park, I guess. I better turn around and get going."

He raised a hand. "Best you drive down to the end and turn. People here don't like you using their driveways."

Marigold gave the officious old duffer a dismissive wave, drove ahead to the turnabout, home for the garbage dumpster more like, reversed direction and started back toward the entrance. As she came up on the Airstream she noticed another vehicle parked behind it, out of sight if you were driving in from the road.

Outside the gate she pulled out her phone. "Lyle, what does Bigelow drive?"

"A honkin' black crew cab. Fat fenders, knobbly tires, plate number BIG1. Why?"

"Because I just drove by your friend Lee's trailer, and guess what I spotted round the back?"

"You better call 911 then."

*

Way to go Marigold! Quite the story for her. Come on, you so-called law enforcers, get the lead out.

Moments later, Harrington and Sergeant Wowchuk hustled past the door of the conference room door, pulling on vests like the ones Laura had found in the shed. Laura, Garth and their parents followed.

Monty looked put out. "We have no idea what's going on. The Chief got a call and they dropped everything."

"Marigold's found Bigelow," Lyle answered. "She just called me. His truck's out at Lee's place."

Sergeant Wowchuk rolled his eyes and swore under his breath.

Garth looked pissed off too. Lyle got up and went over. "Hey, you," he asked, "what's shakin'?"

"Nothing."

Still got a pole up his butt over Laura. "Hey, we get to skip school. Wanna go to your place and play Warcraft after this?"

"Possibly, but I have to walk Ranger first."

Dr MacDonald raised a hand. "Just a minute, can we sit?" Everybody sat, Monty next to Dr MacDonald, like two judges about to render a verdict. Or a sentence. Or both. Lyle slumped down beside Mom. Oh great, here comes the "something else" they wanted to talk about.

"Lyle, you've saved lives," MacDonald said. "It was heroic and nothing can take away from that. But then none of it would have happened, would it, if you hadn't got that reporter woman to take you out to that barn in the first place?"

Monty interrupted. "Jim, we've been over this, let's get to it now, please. Lyle, we've been thinking about how to thank you."

MacDonald took a moment. Then, "Lyle, Laura told us you want a career with the police, is that right?"

Laura spoke up. "Of course it's right, Dad. He told me, I didn't make it up."

Jeez, this had come out of nowhere. Mom was staring at Lyle like, what? Answer the question, dummy, he told himself, make up your mind. Step across a line, like in Warcraft, no going back. Head for something different than the garbage life he'd pictured in the tunnel? Absolutely. He'd already made that decision during last night's showdown with Brad. So say the truth. "Yes, I could do that."

"Well then, Lyle," MacDonald said, "if your mother agrees, Monty and I would like to pay for Police College. There's grants and such but we'll cover the rest, including living expenses. But you have to graduate high school and clean up your act, because everybody knows you've been in some scrapes. They won't take you otherwise."

Monty nodded agreement. "Judy, you know I think a lot of Lyle. I'm sure the two of you will need to talk it over. We want to do something meaningful here, so can you let us know when you've decided?"

Judy shook her head like that wasn't necessary. "Lyle, you want to do this? 'Cos if you do, I'm good with it."

Laura gave Lyle a big grin and a go-for-it thumbs up. Mom's gaze was level, and proud at the same time.

Dr MacDonald cleared his throat, not looking Lyle in the eye. Or anybody. "There is one more thing."

Uh, Oh. Here came the conditions in fine print. It hadn't taken long.

"You see, Lyle, we're a little bit concerned, my wife and I. The last couple of days have obviously drawn you and Laura close. We just think it's rather soon. It's understandable but, well, we don't think it's the right time for you two to——"

"Dad, are you in on this?" Laura, wide eyed, looked ready to explode, but the interruption came from another direction, a scraping noise as Garth shoved his chair back and stood.

"Not our affair, son. Sit down." Monty shook his head, embarrassed.

Garth wasn't having it. "Dad, I can't believe what I just heard. This is so not right. Talk about parental overreach. It's stupid. Kids at school, they get to like each other and what's the problem? Parents telling them they can't be friends? That is so, like, fifty years ago. Are we in a time warp here?"

Monty stared at Garth. Clearly Garth had just blown him away. Lyle felt like giving him a fist pump. Monty made a zip-it gesture but Garth still wasn't done.

"Lyle is my friend, my only friend if you want to know, 'cos everybody else thinks I'm weird but Lyle treats me like I'm normal." His voice started shaking. "And I'm not stupid, I know I'm not your average kid but like I said, he hangs out with me anyway, so…" He ran out of words and sat down.

Could you ever really know Garth? The guy'd been sulking barely a minute ago because, if Lyle guessed right, he was scared of losing his only friend to a girl who'd stolen that friend's heart, an old-fashioned phrase but it fit. Didn't he understand that friends came in separate compartments, guy friends, girlfriends, the one not crowding out the other?

Guess not, but here he was anyway, standing up for Lyle like he had on the snow-covered track at the Falconers'. It occurred to Lyle that you never knew what was going on inside other people's heads. You might think you did but you didn't. You were alone in there, peering out at the world through two video-cameras called eyes. He wasn't sure how he felt about that, sitting in a drab conference room on a winter morning at the cop shop in Southmead, Huron County, Ontario.

The flush of indignation was still on Laura's cheeks, but she had her emotions in control. "Dad, since you're so dead set against me seeing Lyle, there's something else you and Mom better know. I really didn't want to tell this, but now I have to. There's another time Lyle rescued me, Garth as well, when they picked me up at Darlene's."

Her father stared at his hands and gave a slow shake of the head like he'd had all the teenage drama he could handle.

Laura ignored it. She explained how Darlene's Dad had found her and taken her phone. MacDonald's palm slapped the table. "Wait a minute, this is crazy! You told us you lost your phone. Why on Earth would he take it? Is this the truth now Laura? Because we've had it up to here, young lady. Your mother and I have been through hell because of you."

"Don't you talk to her that way," Lyle burst out, "you think you've been through hell? Give me a break! Think about what she went through in that fire, what all of us went through, so back off!"

Monty jumped to his feet and raised his hands. "People, let's all cut each other some slack. What everyone in this room needs now is each other's love and support. Take it easy, Jim, please. Go ahead Laura."

Laura took a shaky breath. "He said he was taking me somewhere safe. But what it was, he wanted to keep me from telling anybody about the occupation."

MacDonald still couldn't contain himself. "That's ridiculous! Did he think you wouldn't tell eventually…or was he going to…oh no, oh my God."

"Dad, he'd lost it. I don't think he had a clue what to do with me, I think—"

"Oh, my dear child, never mind what you think. Jesus Christ, that guy is in so much shit." Dr MacDonald reached across to his wife, who was weeping quietly, and clasped her hand.

"So Laura," Monty asked gently, "then what happened?"

"He shoved me in his truck. But then Lyle and Garth and Marigold came and saw. So Lyle, and Garth too, stood and blocked the track, but Mr Falconer wasn't going to stop. He was going to run them down!"

Lyle spoke up. "So you grabbed the wheel, didn't you, and the truck went in the snowbank and he ran off. What it comes down to is we saved each other." He turned to his friend. "And Garth, buddy, that was pretty outstanding how you came and stood by me there. I thought it was game over."

The room went silent. Eventually Laura spoke. "Mom and Dad, I don't want to talk about this whole thing anymore, not now, I honestly don't."

What did that mean? Had she changed her mind and decided he was nothing but trouble and attitude after all?

Embarrassment lined Dr MacDonald's face. "I'm so sorry sweetheart, you've been through so much. Alright, we can address this another time."

No way. Lyle couldn't leave not knowing. Any moment he expected a conniption from Mom but she sat expressionless, apart from her eyes. They gleamed alert and expectant, and what they told him was, "Son of mine, you just grew up. This is your call."

"No," he said, "we have to finish this now. Dr MacDonald, what you're saying is, you'll pay for Police College if I stay away from your daughter. You know what? If that's the deal, you can keep it. Like, I appreciate the offer but it's not up to me. If Laura wants to hang out with me, I'll be there for her. I mean, what kind of a wimp would take that deal? And if she doesn't like me after all, you wasted your money."

MacDonald turned and locked eyes with his wife. She sniffed and wiped away a tear with a finger. "Oh, Lyle," she said, "I am so very sorry. We've made such a huge, huge mistake here. You are obviously not the young man we thought you were. Our apologies to you and your mother both, because we have insulted you this morning. What must you think of us?"

Lyle cringed and willed Mom not to answer that.

Laura's mother wasn't done. "Lyle, forget what we said about you not seeing our daughter. Please do take our offer. Get accepted for Police College, and the money will be there. We'll put it in trust right away."

"And if he wants do something else?" Mom asked, getting down to practicalities.

"Same thing, as long as he graduates high school. Yes, Lyle?"

"Yes, and thank you. And if Laura still wants to hang out, I promise to treat her proper, honest. And I…" He started to say more, but the turmoil in his brain had his voice shaking like Garth's, so he didn't. Laura looked over and gave him a tired smile. Was it going to be alright?

The hour was past noon. The parental units agreed on a pub lunch. The teenagers chose Gino's Pizza. Exiting to the parking lot, everyone bundled up against the cold. The Niles BMW was long gone.

Garth beckoned to Lyle. "You go on. I have to get home and walk Ranger." He didn't wait for a reply and, though still unsure about where his friend was at with the Laura thing, Lyle appreciated the gesture. He'd never been alone with Laura, just the two of them. They hardly knew each other really. Weird, so much to look forward to learning and sharing, but something told him they already knew the stuff that mattered.

Leaving the parking lot, Lyle took Laura's hand in a tentative grasp. She squeezed back and held on. It *was* going to be alright, and here they were at last on Main Street, Southmead, not a total dump conceivably, holding hands, going for Pizza.

29. BROTHERS

Back to the regular morning routine: get yelled at by Mom to move it; a token shower followed by a shave Lyle didn't really need. He was pulling on underwear — clean today, woohoo — when his phone chimed, text incoming.

Sender: Laura. *Check out InsideHuron website. c u in school. Pizza was awesome. Xoxoxoxo.*

Awesome it had been, especially the make-out session out back of Gino's. Had he dreamt it? No, the memory was real, Cloud Nine real. And what Lyle remembered beyond everything was the intensity in Laura's eyes as she'd pulled him in for the never-going-to-happen kiss he'd imagined outside Van Beek's Hardware the day it had all started. Those wide blue eyes had looked right into his head.

He brought up the browser on the phone.

INSIDEHURON.COM

Connected to the Huron Beacon

Arrest Made in Connection With Sunrise Fire

Police Seek Persons of Interest

Marigold Wallace, Senior Reporter

In custody today is Mitchell Bigelow of Lorne Township. The arrest follows inquiries by Southmead Police into Sunday's fatal fire at Sunrise Foods. Deceased in the fire was Bradley Watts, also of Lorne Township.

Police have named three persons of interest in their investigations: William Niles, Manager of the South Huron Farmers' Co-operative, Warren McKaskell, President of Sunrise Foods, and Bertram Falconer, employee at the Sunrise plant.

Sources that cannot be named suggest information gleaned from Bigelow has raised Police interest in the three men, who have so far not been located.

Sources also suggest that the Sunrise fire was deliberately set, and that acts of heroism averted further fatalities.

Anyone having information that may assist the police investigation is encouraged to call Southmead Police or 1 800 222 TIPS.

This is a developing story. Check back for updates.

So Brad hadn't made it out. What to think? Lyle wasn't sure Brad even knew a fire was planned. He'd meant to lock Lyle up with the prisoners, except he hadn't. He'd run off instead. What to feel? It kind of sucked. But then Lyle remembered Mr Park bleeding on the floor of his store and the sucking didn't last. And this guy McKaskell? There you go Marigold, the payoff guy, like you said.

Mom hustled in and set about changing the dressing on his knee. Lower down, the cast was starting to itch like crazy. Nothing to be done about that, deal with it. Next came instant oatmeal in front of the local news. Nothing about the fire they didn't already know, but then the presenter brought up the search for persons of interest.

Mom put down her coffee, grabbed the remote and turned off the TV. "Lyle," she said, "come over here."

Why the resignation on her face? Mom should be doing a happy dance today but instead she had the look of somebody heading off to the dentist. Lyle went over and sat on the arm of the sofa.

"Son," Mom gripped a copy of *People Magazine,* screwing it into a tight roll, "I need to tell you something you were never supposed to know. But because of all that's happened I have no choice."

Whatever, Mom, he thought, you've made your choice, so spill it.

"Lyle, when Billy Niles called and offered to renew my lease, he threatened me as well. Oh Lyle, he threatened to tell you is that Dad is not your real father, and it's true, he's not."

Major head rush. Lyle felt himself standing back watching Mom talk to some nameless kid.

"Billy thinks his brother Hank was your father. Hank told him, I guess, and I did see Hank for a spell back then. He was a very different guy. He made me laugh, scared me a bit as well, and we had a fling. These things happen, Lyle. But he's not your father."

Mom pitched *People*, reached out and gripped Lyle's hand like she had at the station yesterday. "Niles said he'd tell you if things went bad for him. And now they have, haven't they, with the cops after him and all? I guess Bigelow sold Niles out so they'd go easy on him."

Go easy? Unlikely, but the thought hauled Lyle back from wherever his head had gone. "Mom, forget Bigelow. Who is it?"

Not Hank Niles, which was a total effin' relief, so who? Then, in the way memories had started surfacing out of nowhere lately, Lyle recalled how Mom had pushed him to pal up with Garth, and the undeniable yet inexplicable way the pair of them had hit it off. And he knew, surprised that he hadn't known sooner.

"Mom, shut up. It's Monty, isn't it?"

Mom nodded.

Questions. Garth was his half-brother. Cool, no problem, but did Monty know, or Dad who wasn't Dad, except oh yes he was and always would be? He had to ask.

"Monty knows," Mom replied, "nobody else. Can we keep it that way for now?"

"Sure, Mom, stuff happens alright? I get it." Other questions could wait. Nothing wrong with having two fathers. Double cash donations at Christmas and birthdays? He could handle that.

Hoping to avoid boohooing, Lyle explained this to Mom. It didn't work.

The school bus was due. He'd made promises, no more skipping class or getting sent home for attitude. Lyle shoved his school stuff in his backpack, pulled on his parka and made it to the curb as the bus — Sandy at the wheel as usual — shuddered to a stop. Lyle climbed aboard and took his customary seat four back on the left. The door sucked shut, Sandy mashed the transmission selector and the bus ground into motion. Everything the same as every other day, except in some weird way not. Not at all.

The bus bumped across the tracks. Lyle remembered that other time he'd crossed them, on his bike under an amazing star-filled sky, the night he'd embraced his mission and nearly got himself killed like an idiot. He wondered what Kenny would think of him now and had a moment of aching sadness for his lost big brother.

Through town, everywhere was still quiet. They came up on the PetroCan. Get out of here. A familiar figure patrolled the forecourt. What was Garth doing here this early?

Lyle lurched to his feet. "Sandy, stop the bus, I gotta get off!" Sandy huffed and puffed but she pulled over and cracked the door. "Lyle, I have to keep my schedule."

"No problem Sandy, see you later."

The sneery voice of Troy Thomas sounded from the rear. "Ooh, ooh! He has to go hug his bestie!" Followed by kissing noises. Lyle gave Troy the one-finger salute over his shoulder and stepped off the bus.

A grin arrived on his face of its own accord. "What's up bro? Are you headed to class or, like, standing here trying to look cool?"

"Class, I guess." Garth fell in beside Lyle and they advanced in the general direction of Southmead High, kicking slush around and shoving each other into snowbanks. Past Mr Lube and Al's Plumbing they reached the end of town, school not far now. In the frozen fields, the wind turbines were doing their stranded alien thing, signalling hopefully for a ride home with their slender blades, like always.

Yet the sense of things not the same wouldn't leave. Lyle had to ask. "Bro, the windmills are turning the wrong way. What's with that?"

"Wake up, my brain-challenged friend," Garth replied, "the wind's changed, which you obviously haven't noticed. It's veered round to the South and the windmills have followed it, duh, like they're programmed to. There's a thaw coming."

ABOUT THE AUTHOR

Raised in Bristol, UK, Dave Moores secured a place at Cambridge University where he took a degree in Philosophy. Since prospects for a lucrative career as a philosopher were non-existent, Dave's interests quickly took a hard turn away from liberal arts to technology, resulting in a Diploma in Electronic Engineering from British Aerospace College. His inclination to write was sparked soon after by a short story contest in the industry journal *Airframe.* The entry, a science-fiction piece, didn't win but received publication.

Marriage, the arrival of offspring and, in due course, migration to Canada, took writing off the table. Along the way, Dave's career spanned the domain of information technology, culminating in the position of Chief Systems Architect in a major high-Tech corporation.

Dave has long enjoyed a passion for competitive sailboat racing. One evening after a race, his crew of spirited ladies suggested he write a story based on their adventures and personal anecdotes. The writing gene was reactivated and the result was *Windward Legs*, Dave's first novel, set in the sailing milieu of Ontario's Golden Horseshoe and much enjoyed by the sailing crowd.

Dave's preference, both in reading and writing, favours narratives that keep the pages turning. He's a big believer in one of Elmore Leonard's Ten Rules for Writers: *If it sounds like "Writing," rewrite it.*

Attitude is Dave's second novel. His third, *Sparkles and Karim,* set in Iraq during the ISIS incursions, is coming along.

Dave lives in Oakville, Ontario with his wife Chris and Gemma The Cat, both of whom are dearly loved and keep him on his toes.

MORE BOOKS FROM MIDDLEROAD PUBLISHERS

www.middleroadpublishers.ca

ALL AVAILABLE ON AMAZON

MiddleRoad | Publishers

"Making literature see the light of day."

Racing With The Rain

By Ken Puddicombe

"Ken Puddicombe's brilliant novel...an historic political conflict in Guyana, during the Cold War and the cold cynicism and tragic irony of a state sacrificed to super-power hegemony." -Frank Birbalsingh, author of *Novels and The Nation: Essays in Canadian*

JUNTA

By Ken Puddicombe

"A gripping story (of) an imperfect democracy...the tension...builds increasingly from page to page."—Rico Downer, author of *There Once Was a Little England*

Down Independence Boulevard And Other Stories

by Ken Puddicombe

"A brilliant collection of stories telling the tales of people forced to leave their homes...craving the past, escaping from racial conflicts and dictatorship..."—Judith Kopacsi Gelberger, author of *Heroes Don't Cry*.

Perfect Execution

by Michael Joll.

"Michael Joll is a master of surprise endings, but they never seem forced. He always stays true to his characters and their worlds." —Nancy Kay Clark, author and editor, *CommuterLit.com*

PERSONS OF INTEREST

By Michael Joll

"Exotic and intriguing! Joll brilliantly captures the reader's interest with vivid imagery and a relentless sleuth." —Phyllis Humby, short story writer, poet and novelist.

WITNESSES AND OTHER STORIES

By Raymond Holmes

"Whether comedic or tragic, plunge his readers into vivid slightly askew worlds, where violins hold memories, suitcases vanish, ghosts abound and death waits behind every door."—Nancy Kay Clark, author of *The Prince of Sudland: Escape from the Palace*.

Manufactured by Amazon.ca
Bolton, ON